HIM

A NOVEL
BY

CAREY HEYWOOD

HIM

Cover by Okay Creations
(www.okaycreations.com)
Edited by Yesenia Vargas

ISBN 978-0-9887713-7-6

To Seth. I met you seven years before our first date.
You will always be my HIM.

HIM

Chapter 1

Present

After closing the refrigerator door, I pause, juice in hand, to look at my brother's wedding invitation. It's held up by a local pizza place's magnet and I've looked at it at least a hundred times. I should probably start packing. I'm normally so good at it, always prepared in advance for whatever trip I'm taking. This time is different, I'm headed home. When I got the save the date card a year ago, I called my brother, the groom. I tried to sell Brian on the idea of a destination wedding. Someplace tropic, Aruba or maybe Cabo. No, his fiancée, Christine was set on Decatur, our hometown. Something about dreaming about getting married in the little white church there and having all of her friends and family with her. Ugh.

There is no getting out of going, kind of a requirement of being a sibling. Plus, Christine, the bride, wants me to be a bridesmaid. At least the bridesmaid dresses are pretty, I picture the pale blue dress hanging in my closet. I take a sip of my drink as I walk into the living room. Our condo has an amazing view of the Rockies from the picture window in the living room. Sawyer has her mat laid out in a patch of sunlight in our living room and is going through a series of yoga poses. I sit on the sofa, waiting for her to finish.

After ending in a final child's pose, she turns to me, her gray blue eyes bright. She rolls up her mat before joining me on the sofa, tucking her legs under her as she sits.

"Dude, have you packed yet?"

"Dude?" I cock my head at her. "You never say dude."

She blushes. Sawyer also never blushes.

I pick up a pillow and throw it at her and laugh. "But I know somebody who does!"

"Don't change the subject." She avoids what I've said altogether. "Packed yet?"

I flop back onto the arm of the sofa. "No, I haven't." I groan. "I don't want to go."

I know I'm whining, but I really don't want to go. She stands, holding out her hand to help me off of the sofa, which is laughable considering how much smaller she is than me. "Stop being a wuss." I let her pull me up. "I'll help you pack."

"Fine," I grumble and follow her, my shoulders slumped the whole way to my room.

I tried packing last night and had gotten only as far as pulling down my shiny red rolling suitcase. It still stands, proudly, next to my closet. I lift it and lay it open across my bed. Sawyer buzzes around me, throwing stuff into it.

"I don't think I'll need so many dresses," I argue.

"You never know. Maybe you'll hook up with a groomsman."

I pick up one of the dresses she's flung in my suitcase and neatly refold it. "Unlikely. All but one are married or already have girlfriends."

She smirks, lifting a brow.

"What?" I shrug my shoulders. "I asked Brian last time I talked to him. Even asked him the name of the only single guy, but he had to hang up before he could tell me."

"Why? Were you planning on practicing doodling his name on your binder?"

I roll my eyes. "I don’t do that."

"Right, Sarah. Your last *real* relationship was in high school. Can you repeat after me? High school." She uses air quotes.

"I've dated," I argue weakly.

She gives me a look like, really?

But I'm gaining speed. "Yeah, remember that guy? What was his name? The one who had the three legged dog."

She nods. "That was a really cute dog. If I remember correctly, you spent more time with Rover than Jeremy. And why do I remember the name of the guy you dated and you don't?"

I look away. "Did not."

She keeps going. "So why did you stop seeing Jeremy?"

I lie. "I forget."

Sawyer's always been able to tell when I lie. "Liar! You stopped seeing him because he flossed! Who does that? Who thinks flossing is a con?" she says in disbelief.

"You know that's not why. It's not that he flossed. I like that he flossed. It's that he had to tell me every time he was going to go floss. Why? Why did he do that? Was he trying to prove something? Hey, look at me." I wave my hands in the air. "I'm going to go floss now!"

Sawyer throws a pair of socks at my head. "He was a dentist. You are a crazy person."

I turn to pick up the socks from the floor and put them in the inside pocket of my suitcase "He just wasn't for me." I grin, looking up. "I would've kept his dog, though. His name was Tank by the way."

Sawyer brings my bridesmaid dress out of the closet and sets it on top of everything else, folding it in the middle. "I'm worried about you."

I freeze. "Why?"

She shakes her head. "I know you, and I want you to know I am so proud of everything you have accomplished. But."

I raise a brow. "But?"

She takes a deep breath. "But you are using your job as a reason to not cultivate human relationships."

"What? Human relationships? What are you, a robot?"

"Don't argue. Besides, I predate your company. I'm grandfathered or whatever. And, besides me, who do you talk to or hang out with?"

I spin my ring. "I met Jared for lunch, like..."

She laughs. "Sarah, you had lunch with Jared six months ago. We're going out tonight."

"I can't." I groan. "I have to fly out early. I have that lumber yard account to set up before I go home."

"You aren't flying straight home?"

"No." I shrug. "It's work."

"You need to hire someone else to cut your workload down. This is too much for one person, babe."

"I'm fine. I can do it."

She cuts me off. "Yeah, ‘cause then you couldn't hide behind your job anymore. We're still going out tonight. I'll have you home early."

"Why is this such a big deal?"

"Sarah, when was the last time you had sex?"

"I'm not sleeping with anyone tonight."

"Geez, dude, you need to loosen up."

"Ah ha! You just said dude again."

She waves me off, walking back into my closet and pulling out a green dress. "Go shower and wear this." She sets it on my bed before walking out of my room.

I'm drying my hair when she comes back to check on my progress. Taking my brush from me, she starts playing with my hair. Hair has always been her thing. When I first met her, she had multiple pastel-shaded streaks. I think she's always wished I would let her dye my hair. I, on the other hand, am happy with my brown hair. She braids a chunk of it and pins it like a headband across the top of my head. We head to her car, a Hummer. It always makes me laugh because Sawyer is tiny and her car is huge.

We head to a nearby restaurant bar. There is a live band playing. As we're seated, I notice the bassist nod in Sawyer's direction. "Know him?"

"Oh, that's James. He's cool. He's the one who lives part-time in France. We went out a couple times."

Our server comes by to take our drink orders. Once he's gone, she looks up from her menu. "What are you going to get?"

I shrug. "Clam cakes, or Chicken Kiev. Haven't decided. You?"

"The Portobello Mushroom Pasta looks good. Hey, I forgot to ask where's this lumber yard you're setting up?"

"Just outside Newark. I wonder if anyone we know still lives out there. Helen moved to San Diego."

"Jake's still out there. Want his number? I'm sure he'd meet up for lunch or dinner."

I grin. She's the only person I've ever met who is on good terms with all of her exes. "I'm not going to be there long enough to hang out. Gotta get in, get out, and get to Atlanta."

We order and hang out until our food arrives. The band takes a break, and James and another guy come over to sit with us. As close as James is sitting to Sawyer, I wonder if he hopes they'll hang out later tonight as well. His band mate, the drummer, is named Trent and seems nice enough. They get up once our food comes to go play some more.

"So what'd you think of Trent?"

I hold up my hand as I finish my bite. "He seemed nice."

Her eyes widen. "You don't think he's hot?"

I glance back over to the stage. "I guess. He sure wears a lot of black."

She laughs at me. "Sweetheart, you could find an issue with any guy. Is anyone ever going to be good enough for you?"

I spin my ring, trying not to think about the blue eyes that owned me. "Someday," I hedge. "Who knows."

We have another drink and stay to listen to the band for another hour before heading home. They are still on stage as we leave, and Sawyer catches James' eye as we are walking out and waving bye. I go right to bed when we get home, wondering if Sawyer will have company once James is done playing. She is something. Part of me wishes I could live like she does, so free. Everyone who meets her loves her. God, when Brian came out to visit once, I thought he was going to ask her out. That would have been just weird. He still asks how she's doing every time we talk. She has that effect on people. I, on the other hand, do not. There are no ex-boyfriends trying to track me down. I fall asleep trying to think of anything other than my first love.

Chapter 2

Past

It's our last day of school before spring break. I've already stopped by my locker and am sitting on the floor next to Will as he rummages through his locker for something. Once he shuts the door, I stand.

Click.

"Will, come on." I cover my face.

"Just one more picture," he pleads.

I protest but only halfheartedly. I can't say no to him, especially when he pouts. I can see his lips through the mesh of my fingers, his full, perfect lips. What I would give to feel them on mine. He has a girlfriend, I remind myself, before dropping my hands. I look right at him, and at the last second, cross my eyes.

"Dork." He still takes a picture.

"What? Is there something wrong with my face?" I uncross my eyes and blink a few times.

He snaps another picture and sticks his tongue out at me as he puts his camera in its case and the case into his backpack.

"So, will you come?" Will asks, giving me that lopsided grin I can't say no to.

"Of course." I fake as much enthusiasm as possible.

Crap. He's chewing on the corner of his bottom lip. He always does that when he's thinking. Maybe he's onto me.

I exhale. "I just don't think Jessica likes me." I look at my feet.

"She doesn't," he admits.

My mouth drops open, and my eyes flick to his. "Then why do you want me to go?"

He shrugs, his typical non-answer. He closes his locker and picks up his bookbag as we make our way to the side exit.

I knew it. "Why doesn't she like me?"

He's shaking his head. "Don't worry about her. She's just jealous of you."

I stop walking, stunned. "Why?"

He rolls his eyes, and I punch him in the arm.

"You're so violent," he grins, rubbing the spot I punched.

I raise my brows. He still hasn't answered my question.

He groans, tugging on my arm so I start walking again. "Fine, whatever. She thinks I'd rather hang out with you."

I wrinkle my nose at him. We both know he would. I have no idea why he's even dating her. She's such a bitch. Will's looking everywhere but at me. Sometimes he seriously sucks at just spitting something out.

"So." I stop again. My hands are on my hips. "You freely admit your girlfriend doesn't like me, but you still want me to go to the movies with the two of you and be a third wheel?"

He nods like he's thrilled I've finally figured out one plus one equals two.

"William Ethan Price." I pause between each part of his name. He totally hates it when I say his whole name. "You are like need-to-go-to-a-mental-institution crazy if you think I'm going to go see a movie with you two."

He turns to me, grabbing my hand, and holds it in both of his. "Please Sarah. Come on. You know you want to see this movie."

I can't lie. I am completely affected by his touch. I am almost tingling all over just because he's holding my hand. Get it together, you pathetic loser, I tell myself, but he's won. I just can't say no to him. No matter how much it breaks my heart to see him with her, I'd do anything for him. Sometimes you just can't help it when you're in love with your best friend, and he has no idea.

"You're paying, and I want an Icee," I grumble.

He grins and gives the back of my hand an exaggerated kiss. My eyes widen as I feel his perfect lips on my skin. I think I must have forgotten how to breathe because suddenly I'm somehow choking on air. Will drops my hand and thumps me on the back. How romantic. Not that I should be even wasting my time thinking about romance. He's not mine.

"I still don't get why you want me to go." I say, once I'm able to speak again.

"Honestly, I wish Jessica wasn't going," he mumbles.

I smack his arm again. "You're the one who's dating her," I exclaim.

"I'm thinking about breaking up with her."

Do it! Do it! My brain shrieks.

"So do you think I should?" He looks at me, chewing the corner of his mouth.

Yes! "Look, Will. I feel really weird giving you advice on something like this. I mean, come on. I have like zero dating experience."

"I think I like someone else."

No! "Who?" I can't look at him. This conversation is like a roller coaster ride. First, he tells me he's thinking about breaking up with Jessica, and now, he might like someone else. I don't know if my heart can handle watching him date someone new all over again.

He hasn't answered. "Who is she?" I keep my eyes forward and nudge his toe.

"I don't want to say. I don't think she likes me like that."

My eyes snap to his. How is that even possible? He is only the sweetest, most wonderful, not to mention gorgeous, guy in our school. Scratch that. State. "Then she doesn't deserve you."

He's chewing on the side of his bottom lip again. He pauses and shrugs before putting me in a headlock and walking like that with me down the hall. In vain I try to push off his stomach, but he just laughs and keeps walking. He is so annoying sometimes. Turning my face towards his bicep, I lick it. He releases me with a stunned look on his face. I stretch my neck and stick my tongue out at him.

"I can't believe you just licked my arm," he stammers.

"You deserved it," I taunt.

"Oh, I'm so going to get you," he says right before he rushes me.

I scream, running out the door and into the school parking lot. Will is hot on my heels. I just barely make it to his car and drop my backpack on top of the trunk. His pace has slowed, and he lazily drops his on the hood. He has a very devious glint in his eyes.

I'm in trouble, big time trouble. He starts towards the back of the car.

I head towards the front of the car, saying, "Please don't, please don't." I have no idea what he has planned, and I don't want to find out.

He's rubbing his hands together and doing his best impression of an evil laugh. It's making me laugh, and I kind of have to pee. This is bad.

"Promise you won't tickle me," I beg.

"No promises, Miller Lite." He moves closer.

I scream again and am at the back of his Jetta again.

"Gotta face the music, Sarah. There's no way you're getting out of this."

He lunges for me, but I evade him by inches, just feeling the movement of air from his missed grasp on the back of my legs. I'm panting by the time I reach the front of the car. I look back at him and freeze. He's not there. Shit! Where the hell did he go? I crouch down to look under the car and don't hear him until it's too late, and I'm airborne. Before I know it, I'm hanging over his shoulder, and he is racing to the field behind the parking lot. He flops me down on my back and sits on me straddle-style.

"Oh my God," I yell. "You're crushing me."

He just grins and waggles his fingers at me.

I try to buck him off of me, but he just laughs. "Don't," I gasp. "I swear I have to pee. If you tickle me while sitting on my bladder, I will never forgive you."

He chews on the side of his bottom lip as he thinks it over. I'm still trying to push him off of me.

"Deal," he says suddenly. "I promise I won't tickle you."

I exhale and then gasp as his face drops to mine.

"Doesn't mean that I won't still have my revenge," he breathes.

We are almost nose to nose. Is he going to kiss me? I'm just about to close my eyes and dissolve into this fantasy when his tongue comes out, and he proceeds to lick the side of my face from chin to temple.

I'm horrified, and I must look it because he falls off of me to one side, laughing.

"Your face." He's having issues breathing. "You should have seen your face."

I push at him and jump up, unable to suppress the involuntary shudder his revenge gives me. It only causes him to laugh even more.

"You are so gross, William," I huff, marching towards his car.

He catches up with me and pulls me into a hug. "You licked me first."

I step on his foot, and he kisses the top of my head and lets me go. Pulling his keys out of his pocket, he unlocks his car. I grab my backpack and sink into the front seat. He throws his backpack in the backseat and gets in. I know he's looking at me, but I ignore him.

He pushes my knee, and I shake my head, still refusing to look at him.

"Ah, come on, Sarah. Don't be mad at me," he pleads.

I huff and cross my arms over my chest. I'm trying my best to stay mad at him. It never lasts long, but he's making it easier right now because he still hasn't stopped laughing. He licked my face. Ugh. What bothers me the most is for a spilt second I thought he was going to kiss me. I am probably more angry at myself than anything else. How could I even think that? I'm such an idiot.

"Wanna press the button?"

I snort. He seriously thinks pressing the sunroof button is going to make everything all better?

"Well if you don't want to, I will." He raises his hand.

"No, I'll press it," I shout, pushing his hand away and pressing the button.

I wrinkle my nose at him. Damn him. He knows I love pressing that button. I look over at him. He's holding back a laugh. I can tell. I roll my eyes and smile at him. I can never stay mad at him. He grins at me and parks in front of my house. I dash inside and straight to the bathroom. It's a miracle I didn't pee when he sat on me. After I wash my hands, I wash my face, my just licked face. He is such a punk. When I come out of the bathroom, he is leaning on the wall opposite of it, grinning at me. I roll my eyes at him, and he follows me into our kitchen. I pop some popcorn, and we go sprawl out on the sofa in the family room to watch TV. He sits up when his phone rings.

"Hey."

I mouth, who is it? He mouths back, Jessica. Ugh, I hate her. I look away, but I can't help but listen to what he's saying.

"You didn't have to do that." He looks at me.

I shrug.

"But I don't think she even likes him."

I look at him out of the corner of my eye. He's staring at me and messing with his hair. I mouth at him, what? He shakes his head. I take out my phone and check my horoscope, Taurus. Love is in the air. If you are in a relationship you'll find yourself feeling closer to that special someone. Single love awaits on the horizon. Once I'm done reading mine, I read Will's, Capricorn. Your imagination is on overdrive today. Relax, take a step back, and reevaluate your goals. It is possible something has changed that will realign your future plans.

"Alright, fine, I'll ask her." He puts his other hand over the mouth of the phone. "Jessica invited Kyle to come to the movies as your, um, date."

My eyes widen.

"I can just tell her you don't like him, and he doesn't have to come."

My brows come together. "Kyle Nelson?"

He chews the side of his bottom lip and nods.

"I'm okay going with Kyle."

Will looks at me as though I started speaking in tongues. I smack his knee and point to his phone.

He looks at me again before lifting his phone back to his ear. "Yeah, Sarah says that's cool." He pauses as she speaks. "No, I'll drive. There's no point taking two cars." He's looking at me again. I make a face at him, and he smiles.

After Will hangs up, he stares at me.

"What?"

"I didn't know you liked Kyle."

I shrug "He's okay, I guess. I've never really hung out with him. Besides, I hate being the third wheel to you and whatever girl you end up dating. Maybe it'd be nice to have someone too."

"You never feel like a third wheel to me."

I roll my eyes. There's no way he could understand. I turn onto my side, pulling the popcorn bowl in front of me and stretching my legs out onto Will's lap. He leans back and puts his feet on the coffee table, his hands resting on my calves. Every so often he taps on my leg, a signal that he wants popcorn, and I turn to toss a couple in his direction. He's very good at catching them and always has the cutest oh yeah face after he does it.

"Are you wearing underwear?"

I'm amazed that my eyes are still actually in their sockets. I turn my head, incredulous. "Excuse me?"

"I can totally see your butt cheek."

My mouth drops as my hand moves to press down the back of my shorts. I guess somehow they rode up when I laid down. "Yes, I'm wearing underwear."

He shakes his head, looking at my hand as it presses my shorts to my skin. "It didn't look like it."

"Stop looking at my butt."

"Who's looking at your butt?"

Both of our heads turn to my brother, Brian, as he walks into the family room.

"Will is." I'm a total tattle tale.

Brian gives Will a weird look and goes to sit in a side chair closer to Will's side of the couch. He smacks Will across the top of his head as he walks past him, then points at him, then me, then back at him. Will nods, rubbing his head. It was like a whole conversation passed between them. I roll my eyes and pull the throw blanket off of the back of the couch, draping it over my torso and butt. Will just looks traumatized and keeps looking over at my brother every so often. He doesn't relax until Brian declares we are watching stupid shit and leaves the room.

As soon as he is gone, Will looks at me. "Holy shit, I thought he was going to kick my ass there for a second."

I cover my mouth to stop from laughing. "How's your head?"

He raises one brow at me, rubbing his head. "You think that's funny?"

He reaches over to move the bowl of popcorn to the coffee table before grabbing my feet and tickling them. I'm kicking wildly trying to get away, but he has a vice grip on my ankles with one hand. Finally, I give up trying to get away. Instead, I manage to roll up onto him so I can tickle him back. He releases my ankles when my fingertips push into his armpits. He tries to get away, but I'm pretty much in his lap at this point. Will tenses his arms close to his sides so I can't even wiggle my fingers but I can't remove them either.

I tilt my head at him. "Relax, Will."

"Nope, you're untrustworthy."

I grin. He knows me too well. The second I would have been able to move my fingers I was going to tickle him some more but, out of nowhere, he stands and plops me on my end of the couch, quickly sitting back down and covering himself with the throw blanket. What the hell? I give him a look. He shrugs, looking straight ahead.

"Are you cold?"

He doesn't say anything, just nods. I readjust my shorts in the hopes of eliminating any gaps. I can see him watching me out of the corner of his eye.

"What?" I ask. "You took my blanket."

Will shifts in his seat before he balls it up and tosses it at me, hitting me in the face.

"You suck."

He grins.

Chapter 3

Present

"Now boarding Zone Five." The announcement sounds like it's coming out of one of those fast food drive thru window speakers. I turn toward the sound and stand, reaching into my purse for my boarding pass. They had announced earlier that this was a full flight, so I had already volunteered to have my carry-on checked since I knew they would check it whether I wanted them to or not once I was boarding.

I am heading home. This will be my first visit since after that night. I get in line to board the plane, that slow, awkward shuffle of passing everyone who is already seated. Pausing as the people in front of me find their seats. All the while I chant a hopeful thought within my mind. Please let me sit next to someone normal. Please let me sit next to someone normal.

I am flying home to Atlanta, Georgia. Can you still call a place home if you haven't lived or even visited there in years? I think to myself. Maybe I should call it the place I grew up, but that doesn't feel right either. This trip is a big deal for me. I am something of a workaholic, and I'm taking a whole week off. Work keeps me busy. I like being busy. As long as I am, I don't think about, well, stuff. If I was working right now, I might be flying to Seattle or Chicago or, hell, anywhere else. I relax when I finally make it to my seat.

I'm in 21D, an aisle seat. At least that means I won't be stuck in the middle, fighting for elbow space on both sides. There is an older woman already sitting in 21E, her elbows firmly on both armrests. Great. I sink into my seat, pulling my ereader and a stick of gum out of my purse before stowing it under the seat in front of me. I might be able to read for ten minutes before they announce we have to turn off all electronics. The book I am reading is the latest in a series that I love. It was released the day before, and I am inhaling it.

I am at a really good part when the turn off all electronics light comes on. Groaning, I turn it off and pop my gum into my mouth. I travel frequently for work but still am not any less nervous about flying. I zone out as the attendant goes over the safety procedures. I have heard this before. We are moving, preparing for takeoff. I look around the cabin and cannot help but stare at the man sitting in 20C. I can't see his face, only the back of his head. He has thick dark brown hair, and there is a subtle wave to it that the cabin lights catch. It is run-your-fingers-through-it worthy hair. I don't remember seeing him sitting there when I boarded.

My gaze lingers on his broad shoulder. I can only see the right one. I have to assume the left one matches. He is reading a book, which I find hot. I am enthralled as I watch his fingers lazily turn the next page. His fingers are long, strong, I can see a freckle on the knuckle of his right thumb. Why does that seem familiar? All at once I remember, all those years ago, sixth grade English. It had been the first day of middle school, the blending of four local elementary schools into one cluster of a tween hell. My third period English class had been near my previous class. I was the first person in the room, besides the teacher, and randomly sat in the desk closest to the bookshelves. There was a print book out on each desk, and I was reading it as all my other classmates hurried in before the bell. Just as it rang, he walked in the door.

He was tall, his backpack lazily slung over one shoulder. He had thick brown hair and striking blue eyes, and he was walking straight towards me. I looked around. It felt as though time had slowed, and it was clear that he was having a similar effect on all of the girls in our class. Why was he walking towards me? And then I saw it. The last empty desk in our class was right next to mine. As he sat, he nodded in my direction. I can't be sure, but I think I may have been shaking. His backpack was now in his lap as he pulled out a composition notebook. Laying it on his desk, I stared at his hands and noticed the freckle on his right hand for the first time.

The plane jolts forward as we take flight. I am so distracted by the man sitting in front of me, I hardly notice. It just feels so impossible to think that maybe it could be… No, that would be crazy. The possibility makes my mind race. I had left so quickly. There had been so much unsaid. As much as it hurts, there will always be a part of me that wonders where I would be right now if things had turned out differently. Would I be the workaholic I am today? Would I not be single but instead with him? I thought we were so happy. I shake the memory away, still riveted by the person sitting in front of me. He just can't be. I mean, what are the odds? As if he can feel my gaze, he slowly turns his head back to look at me. My mouth falls open. It's him. The goddamned reason I have not been home in seven years just happens to be on my plane. The last time I had seen him was that night. His eyes meet mine, and I watch the recognition pass over them.

"No way. Sarah? Sarah Miller?"

He looks the exactly same but older, bigger. Oh god.

My heart stops. I nod, smiling at him as I lose all ability to speak. You can do this, I think to myself. You can act normal for the next two hours and not like your heart is breaking all over again just looking at him. My tongue feels dry, my gum now a flavorless mass of cement in my mouth. He unbuckles his belt and stands, there? What is he doing? He seems larger than life. Seriously, how had I missed him when I was boarding? He leans over the woman sitting in the aisle seat next to mine.

"Excuse me, ma'am. The young lady next to you happens to be an old friend of mine. Any chance I could I trade seats with you?"

He still has that lazy southern drawl that makes my toes curl. She is older, but he has not lost his effect on women over the years. Her face takes on a dreamy look as she unbuckles her belt and rises. The gentleman next to her in 21B looks at us, then offers to trade with me so we can have seats right next to each other instead of being separated by the aisle. I nod in agreement, already reaching for my purse, still unable to form words. Suddenly, I am in the middle seat I usually dread, but this time, this time I can hardly breathe. The kid sitting in 21A is already asleep, his head leaning up against the window. My purse is still in my lap as he sits. I have to lean towards him as I place it under the seat in front of me.

I can just smell his cologne. To say he smells good is an understatement. I have a physical reaction to his nearness. My stomach flips. Yes, it could be because I am on an airplane, but I know it is him. As I straighten, I blush, some of my hair escapes my clip and is in my eyes. I raise my hand to brush it aside, but his fingers beat mine, and he delicately tucks the errant strand behind my ear. His fingertip just grazes my earlobe. When he lowers his hand, it burns in the absence of his touch. He positions his arm on the aisle rest and rests his head on it, tilting it toward me. I can handle this. This is just a short flight, and then I can go back to pretending Will Price doesn't exist. Who am I kidding? It's been seven years, and I still read his horoscope every day. I can't stop myself from feeling relief when I see he isn't wearing a wedding ring.

He clears his throat and grins at me. "So how have you been, Sarah?"

His smile is infectious.

I gulp. "I've been good. Busy, but good. What about you?"

"Yeah, I'm good. I'm teaching now."

"No way." I could not imagine concentrating with a teacher as hot as him. "What do you teach?"

"Intro to Art." He pauses. "Guess where?" His grin seems impish now, like he is teasing me.

I can play this game. "Back home?"

He nods.

"Let me guess. Renfroe or Decatur?"

"Renfroe. No high school kids for me. Just good ole Carl G. Renfroe Middle School."

The place where it all started. How can someone look so different but exactly the same? Is that even possible? I catch myself staring at his mouth, at the lips that at one time owned me. My heartbreak over losing him had been twofold, since before he even knew I loved him, he had been my best friend. It feels so good to see him, even though I feel the pain of the loss from him in my life all over again. I'm sure what I feel more in that moment. I can't help it. I laugh, covering my mouth with my hand.

His expression seems far away for a moment. "You always had the prettiest laugh, Sarah."

Clear as day, I suddenly remember the time he made me snort root beer through my nose. I roll my eyes at him. Prettiest laugh? Yeah right.

"What?" He looks confused.

"Seriously? You don't remember?"

He shakes his head.

"God." I cover my face. Why am I reminding him of this? I look up. "Does our field trip to the Georgia Aquarium ring any bells?"

His mouth forms an O right before he throws back his head and laughs, soliciting stares from the passengers around us. His eyes are dancing as he struggles to stifle his laughter, chuckling instead. "You snorted and root beer came out your nose."

"You gave me crap for that forever. It was all your fault too."

"How was it my fault? I can't even remember what made you laugh."

"Really?" He shrugs. I make a face. "It was because of the way Mrs. Allen was eating her chips."

He interrupts me, grabbing my hand and squeezing it. "She looked like a chipmunk!"

I laugh, nodding. "I had just taken the biggest gulp when you had to point that out to me."

"Her cheeks. I can't believe I forgot about that." He notices then that my hand is in his and slowly releases it, folding his arms across his chest. "So what kind of work do you do?"

"It's super boring." I cringe, looking up at him before going on. "My company manages retirement plans for small businesses. I get them all set up. Once a business has contracted with us, I fly out to handle all of the initial paperwork."

"Where are you based?"

"Denver."

He chews on the side of his bottom lip. "So what brings you out this way? Work?"

"Nope. Brian is getting married."

"No shit."

I can hardly believe it myself. My big brother had been somewhat of a legend. It was a bit of a shock he was settling down. I have not even met his fiancé, Christine.

"I know, right. I'm looking forward to meeting his fiancé."

"You haven't met her yet?" He looks surprised.

"My work schedule sucks," I say lamely, unable to admit I avoid going home on the chance that I might run into him. The universe has a funny way of punishing me for that by putting us on the same flight. "My mom seems to be taking it well. She can't stop raving about Christine. That's his fiancé's name," I continue.

"Not going crazy over the idea of losing her baby boy."

I nod. "I've heard moms can get a bit crazy over that idea."

He chewed his lip. Growing up, his mother had issues. She went back and forth between being over protective to not even noticing Will, but she had had a good reason for it.

His blue eyes meet mine, and he clears his throat. "My dad passed a couple years ago."

I put my hand on his arm. He glances down at it. "I'm so sorry, Will. I didn't know." Once I had moved away, I made a point to avoid news from home.

"He had a heart attack."

My hand was still on his arm. "How is your mom doing?"

"Not good, you know, but better. I moved in with her after it happened."

"You're a good son."

He shrugs. I slowly pull my hand back, putting it in my lap.

"Can I get you something to drink?"

We both look up at the attendant now next to us.

I ask for a ginger ale, and he gets a cola.

Before taking my first sip, I raise a brow at him. "No making me laugh this time. Deal?"

He smiles, eyes crinkling in the corners. "You still ticklish?"

Back when we were in school, he used to come over all the time. We would watch TV, and he would eat everything in our house. For some reason, he used to always tickle me until I was lying on the floor panting, and then he would sit back down on the sofa like nothing had happened.

I gape at him. "You wouldn't."

He chews his lip like he's thinking it over and reaches out suddenly. I cringe, setting down my drink and bringing my arms up to block him. He chuckles and taps my nose. "Maybe another time."

I exhale, catching his amused look, and roll my eyes.

He looks at my drink. "I only drink ginger ale when I'm sick."

I shrug. "Helps my stomach when I'm flying."

"Motion sickness?"

"Sometimes, a little bit."

He nods. God, this is surreal. I am sitting here, on a plane, talking to him. What are the odds? When he sat next to me in English class, I had felt like the world had shifted on its axis. It was like he had stepped out of one of my dreams. Our teacher, Mrs. Hall started calling out the roll. I remember going stock still, paying attention. I had to know his name. Name after name was called, alphabetically by last name. When my name was called, he looked at me when I said here. I still remember the two names called between mine and his, Kyle Nelson and Mariah Osborne. Then there was his name, William Price.

"Will, here," he had said.

Will.

I blink away the memory. "I'm sorry. What?"

His finger smoothes away a bead of condensation from his glass. "I asked how long you would be in town for?"

I catch myself mimicking his movement on my own glass, pausing when I see him notice. I gulp. "Not long. Just one week."

"Why Denver?"

"Huh?"

He chews on the corner of his lip. "What took you out to Denver?"

Him. I can't say that, but after that night, I did what any self-respecting wuss would do. I ran. "I've only lived there two years. I traveled there for work and liked the city so much I moved there. Before that, I lived in New Jersey with my Uncle Chip. Remember him?'

"Was he the one that used to sneak us beers?"

I nod, grinning. My Uncle Chip is kind of my favorite person on the planet. "He lived out there at the time and had always said I could live with him. He got sick of the cold and moved to Florida before I moved to Denver."

"It was just like one minute you were there and then..." He shrugs.

Why didn't you come after me? That's all I can think as I spin my thumb ring.

He grabs my hand. "I can't believe you still have this ring," he says, looking up at me, eyes wide.

I start at his touch. This is bad, the way my body still reacts to him. I cannot let him do that, even though I want it more than anything else. I pull my hand away from his and cover it with my other hand.

He had given me the ring in ninth grade. He had gotten it out of a quarter vending machine from the Food Lion by my house. He was trying to teach me how to skateboard, and we stopped to get sodas. I had exact change. He had a quarter left over. I told him to buy a gumball, but he bought a ring instead. "Don't say I never got you anything," he had teased, dropping it, still in its plastic bubbled container, down my shirt. He laughed at me while I pulled my hand inside my sleeve to retrieve it. The ring looked like something you would buy from a trendy boutique, not something that came out of a quarter machine. It makes me laugh every time someone asks me where they can buy one. I just shrug and say it was a gift. The ring is a simple plastic one, smooth, with silver and gold squiggles across the top. I treasure it, have worn it on my thumb ever since. I spin it whenever I'm nervous.

"Yep, still have it," I say in a small voice. Time to change the subject. "So what brought you to Newark?"

"This is just a lay over. I was in Vermont. There was this picture I took." He pauses. "It won an award, and the ceremony was there. So what about you?"

I'm not surprised. During school, Will always seemed to have his camera nearby. "That's really cool, Will. Congratulations. Me? I was just wrapping up a retirement plan for a hardware chain."

"Do you like what you do?"

Who asks that? "Um, it pays the bills. Keeps me busy." Self-preservation, keeps me moving.

"Must make it hard to settle down."

I look down at my hands, spinning my ring again. Had he just read my mind? "I guess."

My hair slips out from behind my ear again. When he reaches up, I shake my head, and he lowers his hand. I unclip my hair, and brown waves tumble over my shoulder. It had been damp when I had twisted it up this morning and had dried that way. The smell of my conditioner drifts around me. Will leans toward me, inhaling."Your hair smells really good, like pears. It didn't look this long when you had it up."

"I really need a haircut," I say, examining a chunk. "Can I put my drink on your tray for a minute?"

"Sure."

"I just want to grab a different clip." I lean forward and pull my purse up into my lap. Finding my other clip, I push my hair to the side and pin it, dropping the first clip into my purse before stowing it again.

Will sits there quietly, looking at me.

"We will be making our descent into Hartsfield-Jackson International airport. Local time is two pm and local temperature is eighty-five degrees. Please turn off any electronic devices and wait until the fasten seatbelts light is turned off to move about the cabin. Be cautious opening overhead storage as items may have shifted during the flight," a flight attendant announces over the intercom.

He passes our now empty drinks to the attendant collecting trash.

"Someone picking you up from the airport?"

I shake my head. "I was going to take a cab."

"My car's here. I could take you home."

I gulp. "I wouldn't want to put you out."

"Seriously, Sarah." He tilts his head, giving me an exasperated look.

"Fine, whatever," I mumble.

He elbows me, raising his brows.

"I mean thank you, Will. You are so kind," I deadpan.

"That's more like it," he says, putting up his tray table.

I roll my eyes. Part of me already feels like this is a mistake. Squeezing my eyes shut, I grip the armrest between us as we land, my eyes popping open when I feel his hand cover mine. He looks at me, chewing the side of his mouth. I look down at his hand, his thumb drawing a lazy circle on the side of my pinkie. I tell myself to move my hand. People around us are unbuckling their belts and starting to stand. I don't move for a couple reasons, first one being this far back on the plane there is no point standing until everyone else ahead of us has already gotten up and grabbed their bags. And secondly, because I just don't want him to move his hand from mine.

Chapter 4

Past

"Won't Jessica be pissed that you picked me up first?" I ask, finally getting into Will's car. I'd only had to run back into my house once this time for my chapstick.

He shrugs. Way to non-answer, bucko. Last thing I need tonight is her to be mad at me before we even get to the Multiplex.

He looks at me. "Is that dress new?"

I shake my head.

"I've never seen you wear it."

I laugh. "Because I wear dresses all the time."

"You look nice."

I wait for the punch line, offering one for him when he doesn't provide one. "For a tomboy, right?"

He looks back at me. "You don't look like a tomboy tonight, Miller Lite."

I fiddle with the hem of my dress. Part of me feels like I'm trying too hard. Kyle hadn't even officially asked me out tonight since it was Jessica that set the whole thing up. I was probably reading too much into the whole thing, and he wasn't even interested in me. I just had to hold out hope that someone could occupy the space within my brain where Will resided. Not where he was my friend. He would always be my best friend, but where I held all of my hopes and dreams that someday he would care for me more than just as a friend. I had to accept that wasn't going to happen because, in almost the same breath of mentioning breaking up with Jessica, he threw out there that he liked another girl. That didn't leave much hope for me that he would ever look at me differently.

We drive to Jessica's house first. It really makes no sense that Will picks me up before Jessica or even Kyle for that matter. They all live fairly close to one another. My house is the furthest from his. When he parks, I get out and move to the backseat before he honks. Jessica is all smiles for Will, but they disappear when she sees me. I bet she is wondering why he picked me up first as well. She leans over and kisses Will when she gets in the car. I turn to look out the window so I don't see the kiss, but I still hear it.

After buckling her belt, she turns to me. "Hey, Sarah. I just love your dress." I doubt that, given her tone. "Where'd you get it?"

Great. Jessica and all of her friends all shop at Abercrombie and Nordstrom's. "Um, Target, I think."

I can see Will looking at me through his rearview mirror. When Jessica isn't looking, I stick my tongue out at him and look out my window again. When we pull up to Kyle's house, I start to feel pretty nervous. I'm not even sure why he wants to go with me. Will honks, and we wait for him to come out. He doesn't take long and jogs up to the car. He's not as tall as Will but still taller than me and boyishly cute with his blonde hair and hazel eyes.

"Hey, Sarah," he says getting in, flashing me a smile. He has really straight teeth. "You look really pretty."

I blush, glancing up to meet Will's eyes in the rearview mirror. He's chewing the side of his mouth. I look back at Kyle. "Thank you."

Jessica fiddles with Will's radio on the way to the Multiplex. She stops on a song I know he hates, and I almost giggle. This is going to be interesting. There is a small line to buy tickets. Kyle is standing really close to me. I'm not sure how I feel about it. When it's our turn to buy tickets, it gets awkward when Will tells Kyle he's buying my ticket. Jessica just stands behind him, shooting daggers in my direction. I nervously play with my thumb ring. Kyle, trying to break the tension, asks me about it.

I look at Will. "I love it. Wear it every day."

He grins at me, though his smile fades a bit when Kyle buys me candy and an Icee. Will orders an extra-large popcorn that I know he'll share with me. When we get into the theater, I end up sitting between Will and Kyle. The seats have the kind of armrests that you can push up. My heart starts thumping when Will pushes the one between us up. Then I feel silly when he sets the popcorn there, whispering in my ear that Jessica hates popcorn in my ear. I'm an idiot, I think to myself. I have a kind of cute guy here for me, and all I can think about is how good Will smells and how his breath on my ear makes my pulse race.

There are a couple of times during the movie that we reach for popcorn at the same time. Each time, we look at each other and smile. He has the most beautiful smile. After we eat all of the popcorn, I wonder if he'll lower the armrest. He doesn't, but he moves the now empty container to under his seat. When he sits back up, he rests his hand where the container was, his pinkie just barely touching my thigh. I look at him, but he just stares straight ahead. Will has to know he's touching me. It's barely the side of his finger, but to me it feels like a hot poker, radiating heat all around it.

I have absolutely no idea what is happening in the movie anymore. It is taking all of my willpower to not shift my leg closer to his hand. Maybe he doesn't even know he's touching me. I don't want to risk him moving his hand away. I just want to stay in this moment forever. I'm so preoccupied, I do not realize Kyle is putting his arm around me until Will's face snaps in my direction, and he glares at Kyle's hand. Does that mean? Could it mean? I feel like a horrible person. I have one guy's arm around me, and all I'm thinking about is moving my leg closer to Will, who is sitting next to his girlfriend. Sure, he did say he was thinking about breaking up with her, but had he? No.

It is that thought that makes me finally move my leg, not to, but away from his hand. He looks down at my leg before picking his hand up and putting it in his lap. I should be relieved, but instead, I'm kicking myself for pulling away. There is a part of me that will do anything to be near him. Unfortunately, there is another part of me fighting that desire by reminding me just how pathetic it makes me. I try in vain to get back into the movie, but I can't. I'm almost hyper aware of Kyle's arm around me, and unlike Will's touch, it just makes me feel weird. Plus, his cologne or body spray is bugging me. I'm thrilled once the end credits start rolling.

Kyle reaches for my hand once we are out of our row. I pretend I have to go to the bathroom to get away. Jessica follows me. Great. At least the bathroom is full, so she won't be able to tell that I don't actually have to go. I stand in a stall for a bit before flushing and meeting her at the sinks.

"I think Kyle likes you." She smiles at me.

"Really?" I know he put his arm around me, but he doesn't even know me.

"Yep, and I've heard he's a really good kisser."

My mouth drops. I can't explain it, but even though Kyle seems nice enough, I know in that moment that I have zero interest in kissing him. She must think my expression means the idea excites me because she winks at me and saunters away. I look after her, taking in her perfect hair and clothes. Why do I waste my time pining after Will? I could never compete with her. I can't even imagine how prefect this other girl must be if he's thinking about dumping Jessica for her. I'd like nothing better than to go home and pull my blanket over my head.

Once I make my way over to where they are waiting, Will says the one thing that could make me feel better. "Ice cream?"

I don't want to hold Kyle's hand, so I pretend to look for something in my purse as a way to keep them occupied while we walk to Will's car. We pile in, and Will drives to our favorite ice cream place. We have been going there forever and always get the same thing. It's a bit out of the way, and I'm surprised when Jessica says she's never been there. I look up and catch Will looking at me in the rearview mirror. I'm secretly happy he's never brought her here, until now. Kyle and Jessica check out the menu while Will orders and pays for my cone. I bump my hip into him. He is such a punk. I know he's only doing it to annoy Kyle. I chat with Jim, who works there, while he waits for Kyle and Jessica to make up their minds.

"You kids are graduating this year, right?" he asks.

I nod, finishing my bite.

"So where are you going to school?"

Will has just taken a bite, so I answer for the both of us. "I'm going to Georgia State, and Will's going to the University of Georgia."

"Why aren't you going there too? I can't picture you two going different places."

Jessica's head whips towards Jim, and she walks over to Will, putting her arm around his waist and leaning into him. I have a sudden urge to vomit.

"Don't worry. I'll be there to take care of Will."

I'm already broken up about Will going away to school without me. It is almost too much to think Jessica will be there with him. I'm not the best student, and my parents can't afford to send me away to college. By going to State, I can still live at home and pay for most of it myself from money I have saved up over the years and if I get a part-time job. Also, since I'm a Georgia resident, I qualify for the HOPE scholarship. I just need to save up money before I can think of living anywhere else. Besides, it's only for a couple years. I might have enough saved up by then to transfer to University of Georgia for my junior year.

The campus is only an hour and a half away. I'm hoping I'll still get to see him on weekends and stuff.

Will pays for Jessica and Kyle's ice cream, and we all go outside to eat. Jim mouths sorry to me as I walk out the door. He has no idea. Will is done with his ice cream before anyone else and is quieter than normal, just leaning back in his chair and chewing on the side of his bottom lip. Part of me is judging both Jessica and Kyle for getting their ice cream in bowls. Will and I always get waffle cones. We are clearly the superior ice cream connoisseurs.

Once we are all done with our ice cream, we leave. Kyle asks if we want to hang out at his house, but I pretend like I have a headache. Will says that his mom needs him for something, and Jessica doesn't want to go without Will. Kyle gets dropped off first, and for a brief moment, I wonder if he's going to try and kiss me but instead he gives me a limp hug. My arms stay at my sides as I make no move to hug him back. That doesn't seem to bother him, though, and he asks if he can call me sometime. I freeze before stammering out my number. He waves bye to Jessica and Will as he walks up his driveway.

"I told you he likes you," Jessica says, looking back at me.

I shrug, kind of wishing I hadn't given him my number, even more so when I get a text notification. I pull out my phone.

"Oh my gosh, is that from Kyle?" Jessica gushes.

After checking it, I nod. Jessica is grinning until the car stops, and she realizes we're at her house.

"Babe," she whines. "I thought you were going to drop me off last."

Will shrugs. "We were going right by your house."

"I thought you could come in for a minute." She puts her hand on his leg and pouts.

I start to wonder how my waffle cone will feel coming back up.

He pats her hand with one hand and starts hacking like he's about to lose a lung, covering his mouth with the other. "I think I'm coming down with something. I don’t want to get you sick."

She glances back at me, her face hard. "Okay babe. Call me later." She blows him a kiss and sashays up her driveway, probably shaking her butt on purpose. I stay in the back, thinking it would be super weird to jump into the front seat now.

"Coming up front?"

"Are you sure it's okay?" I watch Jessica's front door close.

"Don’t' be a dork, get up here," he says patting the passenger seat.

I groan before unbuckling my belt and bolting around the car to the front. Will is laughing at me as I practically dive into the front seat and buckle my belt. "Alright, let's go."

"You're crazy, you know that right?" He's shaking his head. "Possibly certifiable." He pronounces the t like tea.

I shrug. I don't know why, but I feel weird about her seeing me in the front seat. It's like I stole her spot. Does not help that the seat is still warm. I'm skeeved out. Will doesn't say anything as we drive to my house, just changes the station back to his favorite.

He starts to turn the music up but stops and looks at me. "How's your head?"

I inhale and spin my ring. "I kinda lied about my head hurting."

I look up at him, and he's grinning. "That's cool, I lied about my mom needing me."

I'm suspicious now. "And your cough?"

He laughs. What a liar, but I lied too so what does that say about me? I'm not surprised when Will gets out and follows me into my house once we get there. He practically lives here. My mom and dad are hanging out in the backyard with my Uncle Chip. Will and I wave at them as we go to camp out in the family room. Brian is already there watching the news. He's in college now and tries to act so grown up. He's three years older than me and goes to State. He thinks he wants to be a lawyer. All I know is, that is a lot more school than I'm interested in.

"Can we watch something interesting?" I grumble.

"This is interesting." He's dead serious.

Will and I just give him blank stares.

"Don't you two even care that Social Security will probably be depleted by the time any of us need it?"

Will's mouth drops open, and I look at him "My room?"

He nods. We head back towards the kitchen since the stairs up to the bedrooms is on the other side of it. My Uncle Chip is in there and slips us each a beer. Will and I thank him before taking off to my room. He flops across my bed as I close the door behind us. My room is small, and it feels even smaller with Will in it. I sit at my desk, spinning the chair to face him as I open my beer.

"I'm going to call Jessica."

"Do you want some privacy?" I ask, getting up.

He smirks at me and shakes his head. "I'm breaking up with her."

I gasp. "I don't want to be in the room while you do that."

"Why not? I thought you didn't like her."

He's right. I should be all over this, but I just can't. Right now I feel bad for her, and even though she has totally done some pretty mean things to me in the past, it just doesn't feel right.

"I just think you should have that conversation face to face. I think you would feel bad after the fact if you hurt her feelings."

He shakes his head, but I can tell he is thinking about what I said. "But her feelings are going to get hurt either way."

"I get that, but don't you want to do what you can to make it not so bad?"

He sits up, opens his beer, and takes a deep swig before leaning back against my pillows. "I thought you didn't like her."

I swivel my chair left and right. "I don't like her, but I still think you should be nice to her." I will not admit how rotten those words feel coming out.

There were times I had dreamed about someone taking Jessica down a few pegs. I let Will think about what I've said while I drink my beer. He laughs when I burp.

I shrug, mumbling, "'Scuse me," before taking another swig. Beer always makes me burpy.

He finishes his beer and makes a basket with his can in my trash can. I jump up, almost dropping my beer. My trash can is right next to my desk, and metal.

"You suck." I walk over and hand him my beer. He finishes it for me as I sit on the other side of my bed. It follows his into the trash can with a bang.

"So are you still going to do it over the phone?"

He chews the side of his lip and shakes his head.

Chapter 5

Present

Will walks with me to baggage claim. It is almost poetic. He doesn't have any checked luggage, only a small duffle-style carryon. As usual, I am the one with baggage both literal and figurative. As a frequent traveler, I normally don't check luggage but given the length of this trip, it is necessary. I secretly have a thrill in being able to use the big rolling suitcase that came with my set for the first time. I love my suitcases. I travel so much I splurged on hard-shelled cherry red ones. We wait near the mouth of the belt. I sense myself wanting to lean into him. This is madness. I first off cannot believe he was on my flight and now the fact that we are standing here, together, right now. We quietly wait for the first bag to drop.

I see him check his watch. "I feel awful for keeping you. Why don't you just go ahead? I can get a cab or figure out MARTA." There is no way I am riding the MARTA train, but maybe it will make Will think I know what I'm doing so he won't feel obligated to give me a ride.

"Sarah." His blue eyes study me. "Don't be silly. I'm not letting you get a cab."

"You're not letting me?"

He smirks at me.

"Fine, wait. Just don't be so bossy."

All at once, I'm in a giant bear hug of his arms. What? God, his chest is absurdly solid, and he smells heavenly. His arms release me, and he grins. "I've really missed you, Sarah."

It is like a punch in the gut. Being here, Will, all of these emotions. I am trying my best to maintain some semblance of composure around him. I say nothing, eyes glued to the mouth of the conveyor belt and nod. I'm too shitless to look into his eyes right now. He is just too familiar. I'm tense. I wonder if I look like a crazy person, all bunched up in the shoulders, standing next to Will with his easy confidence. It must be so simple for him. He's known how to command the attention of a room for as long as I've known him. I had the biggest crush on him during middle school and then high school and maybe now. Shit, don't judge.

He had been so popular at our school, but what really got me was how down to earth he was. We were paired up in English for a project. Our class was assigned a book, and in pairs, we had to create a physical description of the book, write a written report, and give an oral presentation. I still remember the first time he called me. He must have gotten my telephone number out of the school directory. I was rendered mute and could not speak. He thought there was a bad connection, hung up, and called back. Locating my ability to speak the second time around, we made plans for him to come over and work on the project. I had been surprised he didn't want me to go to his house. He seemed adamant about coming to mine.

I was embarrassed by my house and our belongings. I knew he lived in a really nice neighborhood. When he came over, he didn't seem to think anything of it, though, and I stopped worrying about it. He rode his skateboard over every afternoon for a week while we worked on our project. While I didn't feel weird about what he thought about my house by the end of the week, I was still nervous around him. He was so cute, and he always smelled good.

I would catch myself staring across the kitchen table at him, daydreaming about touching his hair. We hadn't presented our project, but on the day we finished our work, I was almost certain he would never call or come over again. I had been stunned when he showed up the next day, just wanting to hang out. Our friendship grew from there. Will played lacrosse and basketball, but otherwise, he seemed to live at my house.

I had random friends, but Will became my best friend. The crank sound of the belt coming to life snaps me back to reality. My suitcase is unfortunately not one of the first out but tumbles down not long after. When Will sees me reach for it, he beats me to it, collecting it instead. Good ole Will. He refuses my attempt to pull my own suitcase, opting to instead place his duffle on top and pull them together. I can see the logic in it, but it still annoys me for some reason. I'm bothered that he seems to be acting like we haven't missed a beat, like there hasn't been seven years since that night. I follow him out to the parking deck. He slows his steps so we can walk side by side.

When we get to his car, I can't help myself. "Another freaking Jetta?"

"They're good cars."

I lean against the side of it and watch him as he loads our luggage into the trunk. "Whatever. Can I press the button?"

He pauses. His eyes flick to mine. "Anytime, Miller Lite."

I wrinkle my nose at him. It seems not falling back into old habits would be harder than I thought. He opens up his duffle, and before I know it, click. My mouth drops, and he just shrugs. He had said on the plane a picture he took won an award. Even though everything else is so different, it is nice to know some things never change. Once we are both seated, I press the button to open the sunroof for old time's sake. As he drives, I am struck by how familiar, and at the same time different, our surroundings feel. We grew up in Decatur, a suburb of Atlanta. It was a beautiful place to grow up. We had four seasons, the crime rate was low, and the schools were good. For a town that was only four square miles, it had a lot going on. Will's neighborhood was much nicer than mine, but compared to the other areas around us, my house was all right.

Will watches me. "They closed the Denny's."

"Shut up." It had been my favorite place to eat. I have always been a breakfast-at-any-time-of-the-day kind of girl.

"Yep, and the Multiplex."

"God, that place was a dump even before I left. Do you have to drive all the way out to the mall now to see a movie?"

"The mall is gone."

"Now you're lying to me." I swat his shoulder. Yikes. It's firm, probably should not have done that.

"No, I'm serious. They're going to build a new open-air one where it was."

I shake my head. "I don't like those. Besides, it rains here too much. What a pain. So, since the mall is also gone, where do you go to the movies?"

"Asking me out?"

I give him a look.

He shrugs and continues. "A new place opened up just north of town. It's not far."

I nod. Do my memories of those places seem any less vivid now that the structures no longer exist? I feel almost sad for the kids that followed us and missed out. Will rambles, which is not like him, the rest of the drive, catching me up on seven years' worth of gossip. I want to tell him I don't care, that I avoid social networks for this reason, but I still love the sound of his voice. It would be silly to silence him. Plus, as he speaks, I become morbidly fascinated by what had become of our former classmates. There were deaths, marriages, divorces, and an unexpected sex change.

"Really?" It was my second really.

"Yep, ran into her at Wegman's."

"More power to her. Gotta do what makes you happy."

"Are you happy?"

"Christ, conversation whiplash."

"That was a dodge, Sarah."

I groan and start spinning my ring. He doesn't get to know if I'm happy or not. That isn't fair. I have made it through so much, all by myself, to get to where I am today. I shrug and look out my window. "I don't think I'm unhappy. Is that close enough?"

He nods.

Let's see how he feels answering it. "So are you happy?"

He chews the corner of his lip. It's distracting, makes me stare at his mouth.

"I'm happy in some aspects of my life but unhappy in others."

"Talk about vague. So what are you doing about the parts that make you unhappy?"

"I'm working on it. I got you in my car again."

Jesus, what did that mean? I have no sane response to that so I drop it, racking my brain for something to say to change the subject.

He takes in my panicked expression. "I just meant that I've missed you in my life."

I missed him too. Most days, I do everything in my power to stay busy in the hope of not thinking about him. Seeing him, being in his car, this will clearly set me back years. When he pulls up to my house, he surprises me when he follows me to the front door after getting my things out of the car.

"Shouldn't you probably be heading home?"

"Nah. I've got time."

Instead of waiting for me to knock, he opens the door and walks right in. I stand on the doorstep, shell-shocked for a beat before walking in after him. He's gone to the kitchen and is hugging my brother and kissing my mother on the cheek.

"What is going on here?' I ask.

"Sarah!" My family rushes to hug and kiss me.

Will leans against my parents' kitchen counter. "Believe it or not, Sarah and I were on the same flight today. I gave her a lift home from the airport."

"What are the odds? How did the ceremony go?" Brian asks.

He picks up an apple from the basket behind him. "It was great. Thanks." He took a bite. He hadn't even asked. What is he doing in my house?

"Seriously, what is going on here?" I ask again.

"What do you mean?" Brian looks at me strangely.

Will shrugs and keeps right on eating the apple.

"He's eating an apple." I point at Will.

Now it's my mother's turn to stare at me. "So?"

Am I going crazy? "Well, why is he so comfortable in your house?"

Will pushes off of the counter, walking around me to throw the core away. "Just because you left doesn't mean I did."

My mouth drops. "You kept coming over here after I moved away?"

My mother walks over to Will and puts her arm around his waist. "Of course he did. Will is like a second son to me."

"I didn't know." I hate how small my voice sounds. I look back up at Will. "So you knew about the wedding?"

Brian laughs. "Shit. He's my best man. He introduced me to Christine."

"Language, Brian." My mother flicks him with a dish towel.

I don't know why I feel like crying. I press my lips tightly together and nod before hurrying off to my room. Will is hot on my heels. I hear my mom call out after us, but I continue up the stairs.

"Why didn't you mention any of this" I make a jerky circle with my hand. "On the plane."

He shrugs. "The element of surprise, I guess."

"So how do you know Christine?"

"She's a math teacher at Renfroe."

I turn to face him and put my hand up on the door frame of my old room. "My brother is marrying a math teacher?"

Will just smirks at me, then nods.

I bend over, clutching my stomach laughing. "He," I say, trying to catch my breath, "hates math."

The look Will is now giving me can only read amused spectator of insane women. God, I feel like an idiot. I hurry the rest of the way into my room and make to shut the door in Will's face. It's a feeble attempt that does not work, so I sigh dramatically and flop onto my bed face down.

"Are you about done yet?"

"With what?" I mumble into my pillow.

I feel the bed lower under his weight and raise my head to look at him.

"Your hissy fit."

I drop my head again. "Nope."

I have clearly been sucked back in time. I'm in my old room, and Will Price is sitting on my bed. Only the last time he was here, we were... I have to stop thinking about the past. I peek up at him, and he laughs but doesn't move. I don't know why I'm so annoyed at him.

I lift my head further and rest my chin on my elbows. "So, on the plane, when you asked where I live and what I do. Did you already know?"

He shrugs. "Some."

I flip over on to my side, my back to him. The whole time I've been gone I just assumed he didn't know where I was or how to get a hold of me. I had always hoped that if he did, he would come after me. Learning that he probably knew where I was the whole time hurt. It only confirmed my leaving after that night had been the right decision. Ugh, why couldn't he just go away?

I stand, backing away from the bed. "I think I'm going to take a shower. You should go hang out with your buddy, the groom."

"I'm comfy."

My eyebrows come together as I glare at him. "Will, you can't stay in here when I take a shower."

"Why not? I used to do it all the time."

"We were friends then." I snap.

He chews on the corner of his bottom lip then stands, walking over to me, pulling me to his chest. "You are still such a punk."

I hate how wonderful my traitorous body feels in his arms. All I want to do is wrap my arms around his neck and kiss the smirk off his face. Instead, in the spirit of self-preservation, I kick his shin. He drops his arms and allows me to push him out the door. I lock it behind him before leaning against it and sliding to the floor. I pluck at the weave of the carpet next to me. What am I going to do? He's a groomsman. There goes pretending like he doesn't exist. Coming home had been a bad idea. It is much easier to pretend like he never broke my heart if I don't have to see him.

I pull my phone out of my pocket and send Sawyer a recap text. I have to grin when I see her picture flashing on my phone moments later.

I don't even say hello. "That's right. On my fucking plane."

"Holy shit, holy shit, holy shit."

I can picture her pacing.

"And he's the best man?"

I groan my response.

"Aw, honey. What are you going to do?"

"I have no fucking clue."

Chapter 6

Past

I stare at my reflection in the mirror. He's single. Last week, Will Price had finally broken up with Jessica Burton. All of these years I had pined over him. Now is my chance to tell him how I feel. We had been friends since we met in Mrs. Hall's English class in seventh grade. Will had never seen me as anything other than a friend. He's the cutest guy in our class. All of the girls want to go out with him, but he had been dating Jessica our entire senior year. I kind of hate her. She's beautiful, her parents are rich, and everyone loves her. Or fears her. Same difference.

I am not beautiful, I'm cute. I don't dress for attention like a lot of the girls at my school for a couple reasons. I am shy, and my parents didn't have a ton of extra money. We do alright. There are kids who are worse off. You just won't see me wearing designer anything because of it. I do have some cute stuff I bought myself, but I'm mainly a t-shirt and jeans girl. I put on some tinted lip gloss, smiling to make sure there isn't any on my teeth. It might sound silly, but I am obsessed with my teeth. I got braces later than most of the kids in my class. My parents just had not been able to afford them earlier. I had also recently gotten contacts when my mom's health insurance changed to include a vision plan.

It is the first day of spring break. Will is picking me up, and I won't have to deal with Jessica anymore. It is opening day for the amusement waterpark. Since it's spring break, most of the kids at our school are going. I have my very first bikini on under my tank top and cut offs. I throw a towel, some sunscreen, my wallet, and cell phone in a small pull-close backpack and run outside when I hear Will honk, only to turn around and run back inside for my keys and sunglasses.

He's shaking his head at me as I climb into his Jetta. "Got everything, Miller Lite?"

I punch his arm. "Shut up."

"Someday I'm going to pick you up, and you will have everything you need the first time."

I roll my eyes and put on my sunglasses before pulling my hair up into a ponytail.

"Alright, William. Whatcha waiting for?"

He gives me a strange look before shifting to reverse and backing out of my driveway. He hates it when I called him William.

"Can I open the sunroof?"

He laughs, nodding. I don't know why, but I love pressing the button.

"Are we picking up anyone else?"

"Nope. You're stuck with me. I expect you to be entertaining the whole drive."

I lean my seat back and put my feet up on the front of the glove box. "God, too much pressure. Just put on some music."

"Actually." He reaches over, pushes my feet down, and opens the glove box, pulling out a CD before shutting it. "My dad got me something to practice my Italian."

He pops the CD in as I put my feet back up. Italy. I don't even want to think about it. His mother's family is originally from Naples. She grew up in the States but goes back once a year to visit family. This year, Will and his dad are going with. They will be gone for a whole month. The CD is an Italian basics language course.

“Hello. Ciao. Hello. Ciao. How are you? Come stai? How are you? Come stai?”

"Do we have to listen to this?" I groan.

He gives me a lopsided grin. "You're just pissed because you're going to miss me."

"Like a hole in the head," I grumble, looking out the window. I don't want to look at him in that moment because he's right. I am kind of devastated he's going away.

He puts his hand on my knee and shakes it. I bite my lip at the contact. "It's still months away."

The rest of the drive, we repeat common Italian phrases. I try to ignore how hot Will sounds when he rolls his r's. When we get to the park, we head straight for the Z section of the parking lot. This is where everyone is supposed to be meeting up. When we get out, I can't help but notice Jessica three cars over, standing really close to Kyle Nelson. Like something is clearly up with them close. I look up at Will. His jaw seems tense. I try and distract him. All I can think is she sure rebounded fast, and I can't help but feel a bit offended that it's with Kyle. Our double date wasn't that long ago.

"So rides first or waterpark?" I already know what he'll say. Will takes his theme parks seriously.

He puts his arm around my shoulders as we walk over to everyone. "Rides first. Always rides first."

Jessica sees us and rolls her eyes. Yep, never liked her. We wait for some more of our classmates to show before descending on the park. Will and I have season passes so we don't have to wait in line with everyone else. He got me my pass as my birthday present this year. I have two presents, funnel cake and my pass. Funnel cake is my favorite and definitely on the agenda for today. Before meeting Will, I had never gone on a roller coaster. I sometimes get motion sickness. Doesn't stop Will from dragging me on every ride, and miraculously, I've never thrown up. I would follow him just about anywhere.

Since school is out, the lines are bad. There seems to be some other schools meeting up here today too. We are waiting in line for one roller coaster. When the line moves, he grabs my hand, pulling me forward to catch up. When we are caught up, though, he doesn't let go. He keeps holding my hand. I have my sunglasses on, so I know he can't see my eyes. I stare at my hand in his. It's not like he never touches me. He does, but in the past, if he had ever grabbed my hand he would have let go by now. He pulls me towards the queue for the first car. That is my Will, a bit of an adrenaline junkie. And he still hasn't let go of my hand.

"So after this one, want to grab some funnel cake?" he asks, leaning down.

I'm not short. He's just tall. Maybe 6' 2" to my 5' 7". "Hells yeah."

He grins, pulling on my ponytail.

"So you two finally hook up?"

We both turn at the sound. It's Jessica and Kyle. She stands twirling a piece of her blonde hair as Kyle fidgets next to her, his hand hesitating before resting on her shoulder.

Will lets go of my hand. "Shut up, Jessica."

"What, you can't tell she's hot for you?" she goes on.

I feel my cheeks redden as I turn around, putting my hands on the gate.

Will looks down at me. "Just leave her alone, Jessica. You know we're just friends."

He can't see my face, but I wince. The next car comes, and I open the gate. He follows me. We sit down and lower the bar.

As the car slowly makes its way up the first drop, he turns to me. "She's such a bitch. You okay?"

I nod, not saying anything.

We're almost at the top. He turns my head to face him. "Come on. Talk to me."

I give him a weak smile. "I'm good." What I don't say is. I'm in love with you.

He shrugs, chewing on the side of his bottom lip. He always does that when he's thinking.

We crest the hill, and he lifts his arms as we take off. He always makes fun of me for always holding on to the safety bar. It's like me in life, too scared to let go.

At the end, we go look at the pictures taken during the ride. The camera is at the bottom of the first hill. Will is looking at me, chewing on his lip. I look sad. He buys it. He has a whole album at home of us on roller coasters. I don't like this picture, but I don't say anything as he slips it into his backpack.

"I'm going to run to the bathroom." My voice is thick as I hurry away from him.

Sunglasses are good for hiding tears. I sit on the toilet, sniffling and blowing my nose. After washing my hands, I splash water on my face and dry my eyes. I reapply sunblock and lip gloss before I walk out. He's sitting on a ledge by some water fountains and stands as I walk over to him. He puts his arm around my shoulders, and we walk over to the funnel cake place.

"My treat."

"Twist my arm." I just don't want him to take his arm away.

He does, though, when the clerk passes us our order. One bottle of water, one cake. We always split them.

"You sure you're good?"

I have a mouthful of cake and wait for it to dissolve before answering. We are sitting in the shade. Our sunglasses are off so I have no way of avoiding his blue eyes.

"I'm good." I lie.

He chews his lip but doesn't say anything else.

We've already gone on all of his favorite rides. "Waterpark?" I ask.

He shakes his head. "When was the last time we rode bumper cars?"

"Like a billion years ago." I laugh.

He's trying to cheer me up. I love bumper cars.

"Well, what are we waiting for?"

I throw away our trash, and we make our way to that end of the park. Halfway, he drapes his arm around my shoulder again. I shiver, and he looks down at me. It's really hot out to get the chills. There is no one in line when we get there so we have the whole track to ourselves. I bee line for a pink car as he calmly strolls over to a green one at the other end.

"I'm coming for you," he teases, pulling the strap over his head.

"You can't catch me," I shout back.

He gives me his lopsided grin and rubs his hands together ominously.

I shiver again, my arms covered in goose bumps.

The music turns on as the cars come alive. I take off only to back track and turn away when he goes the opposite direction that I expect. With all of the empty cars on the track, I have to fight my way through them as he barrels towards me. I scream but manage to get away. I look back at him, and he winks at me. That boy. He comes right up behind me, and I cut over to the right, turning the opposite direction before he can get me again. Now I'm behind him. He grimaces as he tries to get away from me, but it's no use. I laugh loudly as I bump him into the tires lined up the middle of the track. He hangs his head in shame before whipping around to come after me again. This time, I have nowhere to run, and we're nose to nose while he bumps his car into mine. We're both grinning as the music and cars turn off.

"Waterpark?" he asks as we walk out.

"Waterpark!"

We're at a bank of lockers inside the entrance of all the water rides, changing.

When I take off my tank top, he stares at me. "You're wearing a bikini."

I cross my arms over my chest, suddenly shy.

"I've just never seen you in one before," he continues.

"Stop looking at me."

"Sorry." He looks away, putting his hand out for my tank top.

I step out of my shorts and hand him those as well. He pulls his shirt off, and I mentally drool just looking at his chest. I bend down to pull my towel and flip flops out of my bag when I feel a hand smack my ass.

"Who knew Miller had a nice rack?" Josh Jamison, one of Will's friends, jokes.

"JJ, touch my ass again, and I'll chop off your hand," I huff.

"He touched your ass?" Will looks at me. He doesn't give me a chance to answer and gets in JJ's face. "You touched her ass?"

"Chill, man," he says, taking a step back.

"That's not cool. Say you're sorry."

"What?" JJ and I both say at the same time.

Will takes another step towards him, and JJ shrugs.

"Ah, sorry, Sarah. I was only joking."

I peer around Will. "Don’t do it again." I shake my finger at him, but I'm smiling so he can tell I'm not really mad.

He smiles but frowns when he looks back at Will. "I'll see you guys later," he says, taking off.

Will still has his back to me. I grab his arm, surprised by how tense it seems, and pull him back over to the locker. His whole stance and face are just hard, like he's furious.

I tug on his arm. "Will?" He doesn't react. "William."

I see the corner of his mouth pull up a little bit.

"I think I like you better in a one piece."

"What the hell does that mean?" I pick up my backpack and shove it into the locker.

"You just look really nice. I'm seriously thinking about kicking his ass."

"Oh." I knock the side of my hip into his. "It's just JJ. He's harmless."

"He still shouldn’t be touching you."

I groan and roll my eyes.

He shrugs. "Just saying."

"Whatever. Slides, wave pool, or lazy river?"

He chews on the side of his lip. "It was a long," he dips his head on the word long, "walk over here."

"Lazy river it is." I grin. He knows it's my favorite.

We wade into the water, tubes in hand. Once we're floating, he rests his foot on my tube so we stay right by each other. He's never done that before. I'm trying not to read anything into his actions, but I am. It just seems like he's touching me more than normal, and the way he freaked out on JJ, I can't help but feel a tiny spark of something in the pit of my stomach. I'm lost in my own little day dream. I don't even hear him.

"Sarah."

"Yep, sorry."

"What are you going to do when I'm in Italy?"

"Ugh. I don't even want to think about it."

He grins. "You're going miss me."

"Shut up." I look away.

"I wish you could come with."

"What?" My mouth drops, and I look back at him.

"It'd be fun."

"I'm sure your mom would love that."

His mom is not my biggest fan. Probably has more to do with the neighborhood I live in than me but still. Before he had his Jetta, she used to give him crap for riding his skateboard or bike over. She just didn't think it was safe. I offered to go to him, but he didn't like hanging out at his house. It was always kind of weird over there.

"My mom likes you," he halfheartedly argues.

And while I can admit she does not actively dislike me, she most certainly does not like me.

"Doesn't matter. Not going. You'll have to eat extra gelato for me, per favore." I throw please in Italian at the end, remembering his CD.

He drags his fingertips through the water, then flicks some onto me. I wrinkle up my nose at him and remind him this is the lazy river. I know it probably drives him nuts. He's usually always moving, always tapping his fingers, or chewing the side of his bottom lip. He needs to relax. As the river curves around the park, we pass under a small footbridge that leads to the inner part of the park. A group of guys from our school is hanging out on it as we pass under it.

"Hey, Will. Who's that girl?" One of them calls out.

Squinting, I lower my sunglasses to see who it is.

"Oh, shit! That's Sarah Miller."

My cheeks redden as I push my sunglasses back up and cover my face.

"Will, you hitting that?"

He takes his leg off my raft and my mouth drops, but before I can say anything, he reaches out and grabs my hand in front of all of them.

He looks back at them and smirks.

"Damn. Go Price is right, man," another one calls after him.

I pull my hand out of his, and he looks at me like, what?

"You just made them all think we were together."

He drops his head back so the top of it gets wet before sitting back up and looking at me. "I'm just trying to look out for you."

"I don't think I need to be looked after," I grumble.

"God, I wish you wore a one piece. When did you even buy that?"

I feel tears threatening. I am trying so hard not to cry.

"Well?"

"I thought you said I looked nice before."

He flips over on to his stomach and doggy paddles over to me before resting his chin on the edge of my tube, right by my chest. He lowers his sunglasses so I can see his eyes. "You don't look nice. You look fucking hot."

Holy shit.

Chapter 7

Present

"Isn't the point for them to be separate parties?" I lift a brow.

Christine is applying her eye makeup in the bathroom mirror. I was in the shower when she got to the house. Seeing as how I've only known my future sister-in-law for three hours, I know without a doubt she is a doll and perfect for my big brother. She's gorgeous, all willowy with her pale complexion, hair, and blue eyes, almost ethereal looking, especially next to Brian with his perma tan and dark hair. My brother and parents clearly adore her, and it's hard not to. She's confident without being forceful and warm without making it feel overly familiar. She'd thrown me for a loop, though, when she informed me we were going out tonight for her and Brian's joint stag party.

"Just think of it as a rehearsal dinner only for the bridesmaids and groomsmen."

Great, I thought. That means Will would be there. I tap my mouth, looking at the clothes I brought, trying to decide what to wear. I want to look nice, but I don't want to look like I'm trying too hard. I think back to my call with Sawyer, annoyed she talked me out of booking the first flight home. It's only a week, she said. You'll be fine she said. Tonight is going to be my first time seeing him again, and I'm already about to panic. Christine comes to stand next to me. Of course she looks like a goddess in a light grey sheath dress that hugs her small frame. I like a sheath-style dress on top, but I'm too hippy to pull them off on the bottom.

"I think you should wear this one," she says, pulling down a cream wrap dress.

"You don't think it looks too casual?" I argue, gesturing to her dress.

"We'll add a chunky statement necklace. You'll look amazing."

"You wouldn't happen to have a necklace like that with you?" I know I don't.

"Brian gave one to your mom for Christmas that would look perfect with this. I'll go beg her for it."

I laugh, doubting very much that Christine will have to beg. While she's gone, I slip on the dress. It is one of my absolute favorites and fits like a dream.

When she comes back to my room with the necklace, my mouth drops. It's beautiful.

"I know, right?" She laughs, taking in my expression as I turn and lift my hair for her to fasten it around my neck.

I turn to take in my reflection. Wow. The dress is simple. The necklace makes it look elegant. The necklace is four golden chains of clear glass beads. I have some simple gold hoops that will look great with it.

"So how are you doing your hair?"

"Um, probably down. Maybe with the ends curled under. I'm bringing a clip in my purse, though, because I'll probably want to pull it up before the night is over."

"I can curl it while you do your makeup," she offers.

My spidey sense is going off. "Is there a reason I should look so nice tonight?" I ask as innocently as I can.

I can see her stifle a smile, but she shrugs noncommittally. Interesting. This feels like a set up. My only hope is that their intended target isn't Will. I finish applying my makeup before she's done with my hair. While she works, I ask her about how she met my brother. I'm curious what Will's part in the whole thing was.

Her eyes take on a dreamy, faraway look. She was new in town and had befriended Will. They were meeting for coffee one day when Brian saw her. Once he confirmed with Will that she was single, he asked for Will's help with an introduction. They ended up setting up a rouse where Will would meet Christine for dinner only to be called away for some made up emergency, and Brian would step in and have dinner with her instead. That night, after Will left, there were sparks between them from the moment they met. She laughs, telling me how nervous Brian was that night. She didn't learn it was a set up until maybe three months into their relationship.

They were together for a year when they moved in together and then another year before Brian proposed. Earlier, when I first met her, I could tell how happy they made each other. Brian's face was absolutely beaming as he introduced her to me. As happy as I am for my brother, I cannot help but feel a pang of envy at what they have. My own love life is sorely lacking. I dated through college and after. If I'm being honest with myself, I use all of the traveling for my job as a reason to not let anyone get too close. What's the point? I met the love of my life in middle school. Problem is, he hadn't felt the same way.

Christine spritzes my hair with hold spray, and I pull on some bronze, strappy, low-heeled sandals before tucking my clutch under my arm. I can hear conversation in the living room as we approach. My brother and Will are sitting on the sofa, my mother's fussing at my father in the next room. Brian and Will both stand as we enter the room.

"Man, you both clean up good," Brian jokes, walking over to kiss Christine.

"You're not so bad yourself," she replies, straightening his tie.

And she is right. They do look good. When I moved away, they only used to wear jeans or cargos and t-shirts. It's kind of weird seeing my brother and Will in suits. Sure, they'll be wearing tuxes at the wedding, but this is just dinner. My eyes find Will's. He stands quietly next to Brian, and Christine openly watches me.

"So where are we headed?" I ask, mainly to fill the silence.

"This great tapas place downtown. You'll love it," Christine gushes.

"Got everything you need?" Will asks me, his eyes laughing.

I double check my purse and have to run back upstairs to grab my ID, which is in my other wallet. I avoid Will's eyes when I walk back down the stairs. It bugs me that he still knows me so well. Brian holds his arm out to Christine, and she sweetly takes it. Will starts to do the same for me, but I shake my head and hurry after Brian and Christine, leaving him to follow me. It's silly, I know, but I just don't want to get too close to him. I'm only here for a week. There is no point putting myself into a situation where I'll only be hurt. We take Brian's Xterra, and Will and I sit in the back. I can feel his eyes on me. I try to ignore them, resting my elbow on the door handle and looking out the window.

When we get to the restaurant, we are joined by Brian and Christine's other groomsmen and bridesmaids. They're all couples. Great. Seeing as how Will is the only single guy and I'm the only single girl, it is clear we will be paired up for the evening. I don't know why this bothers me so much. It had been great to talk to him on the plane and to feel that rush when I saw him. It's just that once we got to my house and I saw how entwined he is in my family's lives, it annoyed me. He had broken my heart, yet my mother called him a second son and he was going to be the best man at my brother's wedding. How does that happen?

Not that I've ever told anyone other than Sawyer what had really happened that night. Nope. Instead I ran and stayed away from my home and family while he stayed here. It's kind of hard to blame them for liking him, considering they didn't know what he did. Maybe what irks me the most is I caught myself starting to like him all over again. I've always been attracted to him, and these years apart have been kind to him. He isn't the boy I had left behind. He's a man now, a very annoying and sexy all at the same time man.

At the restaurant, I'm seated next to my brother and across from Will. I continue my campaign of disinterest and focus on the plate of spiced oil to dip bread into that is sitting in front of me. I'm hungry, and carbs are one of my favorite food groups. Besides, it would be rude to talk with food in my mouth. We order family style, where the plates are passed around the table and we can all try a bit of everything. Once the waiter leaves with the menus, another waiter offers us tastes of the house sangria. The way he gives the tastes is a bit unorthodox. He goes around the table holding this leather pouch with a metal spout at the opening. We open our mouths, and he squeezes a stream of sangria straight into them from the pouch, a highbrow beer funnel.

It feels provocative, sitting there, my lips parted as Will watches me. I feel myself redden under his gaze. The sangria is delicious, though, so I order a glass and sip it. I jump when I feel Will's leg straighten out under the table and his calf brush against mine. My eyes flick to his. He's smirking. Clearly, he did that on purpose. Tapas are mainly a finger food. Will makes no attempt to hide he is watching me eat. I can't help it, but I start watching him as well. He coats a piece of bread in oil, keeping his eyes on me as he lifts it to his mouth and then licks a stray drop of oil off the tip of his finger. Oh shit, that was hot. I break the eye contact, beating myself up for letting him draw me in.

I excuse myself and go to the ladies' room. Washing my hands, I give myself a little you can do this type pep talk. When I walk out, I see him leaned up against the wall opposite the door.

"Long line for the men's room?" I try to joke, moving past him.

His hand circles my wrist, stopping me. I inhale, frozen in place. My back is to him. I don't try to pull away. I can't move. I just look down at his hand, staring at his damn freckle.

"Sarah."

"What are you playing at, Will?'

"Playing?" He tugs my arm back so I'm facing him. "I promise you this is no game."

"Alright, what do you want from me? Is that better?" I practically spit.

"Everything." He's moved his hands up to hold my biceps. "I want everything from you."

Everything. That one word still breaks my heart when I think back to that night.

My head snaps back as though he's struck me. Don't cry, just don't cry. "I gave you everything once. Now I have nothing left for you."

I pull myself from his grasp and hurry back to the table. When I sit, I glance up to the hallway where he still stands, his eyes haunted. Brian can sense I'm upset. He looks at me with worried eyes. I shake my head. I'm a big girl. There is no point dragging him into anything. It doesn't stop him from shooting worried glances in my direction throughout the meal. Will comes back and sits not long after me. He tries to catch my eye more than once. I can't tell why he seems so confused. He knows what he did.

The plan after dinner is to go to a nearby nightclub. The whole idea makes me very nervous. I just have to get through the night without dancing with Will. Should be easy enough. If all else fails, I'll fake a twisted ankle. When we get to the nightclub, Christine orders shots. I am already feeling buzzed from my sangria and start to refuse until she gives me a pitiful look. I order a glass of water, hoping to keep a clear head. Not that it helps. Brian orders another round of shots next. Christine pulls me and the other girls out onto the dance floor. The DJ plays mainly songs I have heard on the radio. I relax and am having fun dancing and singing along with Christine and her friends.

Some random guys try to approach our group a couple of times, but Christine waves them off, flashing her engagement ring. That only works for so long, and I feel some random guy's hands on my ass. I seriously will never understand the thought process that some of these guys have. Cute girl dancing. Instead of introducing myself and asking if she'd like to dance with me, surprise dry humping her from behind seems like a better move. I am doing my best to politely remove his hands when I see Will approach.

"So sorry, bud. She's with me," he says, coolly taking my hand and leading me to another part of the dance floor.

"I was taking care of it," I huff, pulling my hand from his, annoyed that he doesn't think I can take care of myself.

"I know," he shrugs. "I was just looking for an excuse to dance with you."

"I'm not dancing with you." I turn and walk back to the table.

I can tell he's following me. I pointedly try to ignore him and talk to Brian instead. Brian hesitates for a beat, and I wonder briefly whose side he's on. I give Brian a look and feel Will back away. My traitor body pouts, but this is the smart thing to do. I only have to get through six more days, and then I can pretend like I never even saw him. As soon as I think it, I know it's a lie. He'll still haunt my dreams and make every other guy I've ever tried to date feel inadequate. The only difference is now Will's face in my dreams will be of him now, grown, a man. A very sexy man, unfortunately.

Brian is looking at me in concern. Shit. "Sorry, just zoned out there for a sec. What did you say?"

"Will you help Christine and I put together a video slide show tomorrow? She just found out the place where we're having the rehearsal dinner at can project on a wall during dessert, and I'm crap at that stuff."

"Of course," I say, flagging down our server. When she comes over, I order another water, doing everything in my power to stay clear-headed.

"You okay?" Brian asks.

"I'm great," I lie.

"You just seem so tense. I want this to be fun for everyone. You know, let your hair down. Have fun."

"My hair is down," I argue.

The server is back with my drink. I sip it and turn to watch Christine and her friends dance, mentally mapping out the drive to the local animal shelter back home. It's clear I'm going to end up a crazy spinster thanks to Will. I might as well start collecting cats to complete the picture.

Chapter 8

Past

William Ethan Price has just told me I look fucking hot. I may never breathe normally again. After his unexpected declaration, he casually lifts himself from my raft and floats away like nothing just happened. In fact, for the rest of the day, he acts like he didn't just drop the biggest bomb on me. From the lazy river, we go further into the park to the water slides. I may have forgotten how to breathe again when he grabs my hand and pulls me to a tandem slide. He sits in the tube first, and I hesitate before sitting in front of him, between his legs, my back to his chest. I cringe, wondering if he feels me shiver when his bare chest is on my back. Or if he hears my heart pounding when he wraps his arms around my waist.

I gently lay my hands on his arms, raising them unexpectedly when he removes his arms from my waist. For a moment, I'm wondering what happened until I feel his hands on my shoulders as he pulls me towards him so that I'm lying against him before circling my waist with his arms again. My neck is still stiff, holding my head up. His mouth is at my ear telling me to relax. I close my eyes and lean my head on him, turning my face to look at his neck. I see his jaw flex as he grins. I have never in my life felt this much skin to skin contact with anyone.

All at once, we're flying after the attendant uses his foot to propel our tube down the slide. Will's grip on me tightens as he leans forward, his cheek pressing against mine. We crash into the water a tangle of arms and legs. When I stand and turn my back to him, wiping water from my eyes, I hear him suck in a breath. Then he's behind me again, his body pressed to mine. I look back at him, and my mouth drops when I feel his hands on my ass. I'm about to ask him what he's doing when I feel him adjust my bikini bottom. I blush all over. I guess at some point during our slide, my suit shifted. He looks down at me, and I mouth thank you, his hands still on me. He leans forward, and for a moment, I wonder if he's going to kiss me.

"Get you some, Price!"

We look up. Kyle and Jessica are standing to the side of us.

She glares at Will. "Never knew you had a thing for SPT, Will."

I exhale and step away from him, feeling his fingertips tighten briefly before I'm out of their grasp. SPT. God, I hate that nickname. I may never forgive Mrs. Hall for having that book on her lesson plan, Sarah Plain and Tall. That was the book our class had been assigned to do those team projects on. I hate that book with every fiber of my being. The nickname came the day of our oral presentations and when our physical projects were unveiled. My and Will's project was nothing amazing. We made a cereal box based on the book. It was the diorama of Mariah Osborne and Kelly Sotello that started the whole thing. They had taken my sixth grade class picture and made me the Sarah from the book. With my brown hair and brown eyes, I was plain.

Mrs. Hall made them remove the picture, but the damage had already been done. I was SPT from that point on for the rest of middle school. In high school, the nickname seemed to fade away for the most part. Only the truly evil bitches still broke it out from time to time. Will knows how much it bothers me. Catching up to me, he drapes his arm around my shoulders as we make our way to our towels. Grabbing mine, he wraps it around me. He looks back at Jessica, who is still watching us as he tugs on my towel, pulling me towards him and gently kissing me on my forehead. I look up at him, trying to blink away threatening tears.

"You are not plain. You are beautiful, Sarah, inside and out. She only says those things because she's a jealous cunt."

I give him a wet smile, all the while wondering what Jessica could possibly be jealous of me for. We skip the rest of the slides in favor of the wave pool. We lay our towels out to dry and go in together. This wave pool is huge and has a sandy bottom. I wiggle my toes in the sand and laugh when Will pulls me deeper. Normally, when we come to the park I hang out in the shallower end while Will grabs a boogie board and plays in the big waves. Today, he makes no move to leave me. I bump his hip with mine and nod towards the boards in a silent question. He shrugs and pulls me deeper. The waves aren't huge where we're standing but big enough that we have to jump as they pass to avoid being knocked down. We half-heartedly body surf a couple of them.

When I look at him, I see him chewing on the corner of his mouth. "You okay?"

He looks down at me and gives me a lopsided grin. "I'm great."

He then sweeps my legs out from under me and tosses me into the next wave. He's clutching his stomach as I come up sputtering. I wrinkle my nose at him and charge him, knocking him over best I can. It all seems to be going well until he pulls me down with him. At least this time we both come up sputtering. I make a half-hearted attempt to avoid him when he comes after me. This time, he pulls me to his chest, my hands on his shoulders. I give him a strange look, my eyes widening when I see him close his eyes and hold his breath before he pulls us under. I try to kick away, but he only locks his arms around me tighter. Just when I think he'll never let me go, I realize he's turned on. His arms release me, and we both surface, panting. His face is red. Does he know I felt it?

Neither of us say anything. We just tread water, looking forward for a couple minutes. He's chewing the corner of his lip again. He then takes my hand and starts towards shallow water. When we get out of the water and to our towels, he stretches out face down. I follow suit, loving the way the sun feels on my back. Our faces are turned towards each other. He grins at me before I close my eyes. We are joined by some of our classmates. I fume, watching a couple girls exaggeratingly adjust their bikini tops in front of all the boys. I gasp when cool water drips onto my back and look up to see JJ standing over me.

"What the hell, JJ? You're dripping on me."

Will's head pops up, and he glares at JJ. "Seriously, dude. Back off."

"Chill out, Will. Hey, Sarah. Do you want to come in with me?"

I'm about to say I'm cool when Will cuts me off. "She's good."

I'm fuming and move to stand. "I'd love to."

Will grumbles and gets up to come with us. I can feel his stare hot on my back as I walk with JJ to the water. I've barely put one toe in when I'm suddenly airborne and hanging over Will's shoulder, his hands hot on the back of my thighs. JJ looks pissed, and I mouth sorry as Will carries me further in.

"I can walk, you know," I grumble.

He lowers me slowly so I slide down his body. His eyes are dark, and he's chewing on the corner of his bottom lip.

"What the hell was that, Will?"

He shrugs, his hands still on my waist. I put my hands on his chest to push him away. He only holds on tighter.

Exhaling, he closes his eyes and leans down to rest his forehead on mine. "Why did you have to wear that today?"

"You suck, Will." His eyes pop open. "My suit is way more covered than most of the girls in our class, and I don't see you giving them any grief."

"I just don't like the way other guys are looking at you."

My arms relax, but I don't remove my hands. "Why?"

He turns his head, his breath tickling my ear. "Maybe I want you all for myself."

I'm incapable of speech. My mouth drops open. He lifts his head and studies my expression. I see the corner of his mouth pull up as he slowly lowers his lips to mine. He barely dusts his lips across mine before pressing more firmly.

I jerk back. "Will, what are you doing?"

"I'm trying to kiss you."

I smack his arm.

"Remember when I told you I like someone else?"

I nod, still reeling from the fact that he just kissed me.

"I was talking about you."

"Me?"

He rolls his eyes and pulls me back into his arms.

I push him away. "But why?"

He puts his hands on my shoulders and drops his head down in front of mine. "I've liked you for a long time but just figured you weren't interested in dating anyone. Until you agreed to go out with Kyle."

I shake my head. No way he likes me. "Be serious."

His doesn't say anything, just drops his lips to mine again. This kiss feels serious. I brace my hands on his arms, pressing myself against him. He keeps one arm coiled around my waist and moves the other one up to the back of my neck, pressing my face closer to his. I moan, and his tongue moves into my mouth. My eyes close as the rest of the world fades away. He kisses his way across my cheek to my ear, where he whispers that he has wanted to do that for so long. His mouth moves down to my neck, and it suddenly dawns on me that half of our class is probably watching his performance.

"Will, stop."

"What?" He's nibbling on my earlobe.

"People are watching." I try and step back.

His arm tightens around me again. "Fuck them."

I laugh. "Will."

He pulls back, putting his hands on either side of my face and locking eyes with me. "Seriously, Sarah, Fuck them." He leans back down, giving me a sweet kiss before wrapping his arms around my waist.

"Will?"

"Um hmm." He's running his nose down the side of my ear.

"What does this mean?"

"You're mine."

I snort. "I'm yours?"

"Yep, all mine."

I shiver.

"Are you cold?"

I'm grinning as I shake my head. He drapes his arm around my shoulder as we make our way out of the pool, his fingers brushing back and forth at the top of my arm. I cringe, taking in the expressions of our classmates, most of which are drop-jawed. Will, on the other hand, is grinning and even pops his head towards a couple of people. JJ is back at his towel, shaking his head at us. When we get to our towels, Will grabs mine and again wraps me in it. This time, when he tugs me to him, it's to plant his lips on mine again, right in front of everyone. I'm simultaneously on cloud nine but also sick with worry at what everyone thinks. I try to embrace what he told me in the water. Fuck them.

I slide my hands up out of my towel, letting it slide off my shoulders. He leans further towards me, wrapping his arms around my waist again, but this time, lifting me up so we're face to face. Holding me like that, he rubs the tip of his nose against mine. Trailing a line of kisses to my ear, he asks if I want to get out of here. My stomach flips, and I nod my head. Setting me gently on my feet, we slip on our flip flops and hurriedly towel off. He takes my hand and pulls me away, turning his head to grin at everyone behind us.

"You are terrible." I knock my hip into his.

"You're beautiful," he replies quietly.

We make our way to the lockers and pull on our clothes.

"Where are we going?"

He pauses. "Where would you like to go?"

"Carousel?" I ask innocently.

He rolls his eyes. He hates the carousel, not action packed enough for him. I smile as he grumbles and pulls me towards that end of the park. When we get there, we wait in a small line of little kids. I rub my thumb across the back of his hand, and he smiles down at me before kissing the top of my head. As the line slowly moves forward, I try to wrap my brain about what is happening. I partly wonder if this is just a highly realistic dream, and I'm actually still asleep on my towel by the wave pool.

"Pinch me," I whisper.

"What?" Will looks confused.

I look up at him. "Pinch me so I know I'm not dreaming."

His mouth cracks into a wide grin as he gently puts his lips on mine. Pulling back, he lifts the hand he's holding and places a sweet kiss on that as well before pinching the top of it with his other hand.

"Ouch!"

He kisses my hand again and bends his head to my ear. "It's a dream, but you're not sleeping."

He pushes me forward, and we make our way onto the carousel. I pick a blue pony with a white mane and tail. Instead of getting on one Will stands next to me, his hands on my waist. From my seat, he doesn't have to lean down to kiss me. His mouth is on mine as the music starts. Our kiss only breaks when my horse goes up, his lips finding mine again as soon as I descend. I'm dizzy between his kisses and the heat of his hands on my waist to the up and down and round and round of the carousel. When the ride stops, I take a stumble step and he catches me.

"Will?"

His eyes meet mine.

"Will, what are we doing?"

He looks confused. "What do you mean?"

I close my eyes, terrified of what he may say next but incapable of not asking. "Do you want me to be your girlfriend?"

He pauses. I cringe. Taking in my expression, he tilts his head. "Sarah Lillian Miller, will you please be my girlfriend?"

I'm crying. I can't help it. I've loved this boy since seventh grade. He's always hated it when I cry and begins shushing me and using his thumbs to wipe the tears from my eyes as he places feather light kisses to my lips. "I didn't mean to make you cry."

I plant my face into his chest wrapping my arms around his waist as he plays with my ponytail.

"Hate to trouble you," he says, kissing the top of my head. "But you didn't actually answer my question."

I laugh, tilting my head up to his, putting my hands behind his neck to pull his lips to mine.

"Is that a yes?" he asks against my lips.

"Yes. Now shut up and kiss me."

And he does, slowly and deeply, his hands gripping my hips. My heart is thumping, and at a certain point, I feel like I'm just barely holding on. As though the whole park and the world around it has melted away again and I only exist to be in his arms. We may have kissed for only minutes or it could have been hours. For us, time stood still. When we finally pull back, his hooded expression makes my knees feel weak. My clearly dazed look amuses him. He reaches up to tweak the tip of my nose so I scrunch it at him and stick out my tongue. His eyes drop to my mouth as he licks his lips. Christ, I might swoon.

Shaking his head, he takes my hand in his. "Ice cream?"

I grin. Sure, there are plenty of places we could probably get ice cream at the park, but we never do. There is only one place we ever go to for ice cream. We pass a couple of our classmates on our way out of the park. Our early departure given our very public make out sessions will definitely lead to talk, but I don't care. Like Will said, fuck them.

Chapter 9

Present

Waking up in my childhood bedroom is surreal. Part of me had hoped my parents would keep everything the same, but I guess I could see how having a guest bedroom made more sense. The bed frame and mattress are the same, though. I could recognize those squeaks when I turn over in the middle of the night anywhere. Falling asleep had been hard. Over the years, I have become accustomed to watching TV in bed until I fall asleep. That's what living out of hotels will do to you. Also, I can't stop thinking about Will. Why did he seem like he had unfinished business with me? Did he want to apologize for what he did? I shake my head. As far as I am concerned, if that's what he wanted, I'd rather he choked on it.

That isn't true. Well, maybe a little. Will turning out to be such a big part of this trip had blindsided me. He was the friggin best man. It's a pity, but I'm annoyed he has a bigger role in their wedding than I do. Christine's best friend is her maid of honor, and I'm a bridesmaid. I don't know why that bothers me so much. Plus, it means I'll at the very least have to deal with him during the rehearsal dinner, the wedding, and the reception. I'm not mentally prepared to deal with Will in a tux. I roll over and eye the clock. It's later than I expect so I hurry downstairs. My dad is in the kitchen drinking his third cup of coffee for the day.

"Morning sunshine. Your mother went to the airport to pick up your Uncle Chip."

He tsks at me as I sit on the counter. "We have these new fangled things called chairs. Please try one out."

I roll my eyes and walk over to kiss him on the top of the head, surprised when I notice how thin his hair is up there. I mentally do the math, trying to remember the last time I saw my parents in Denver. It must have been only a year ago. I'd give him crap about it, but he had always been so vain about his thick brown hair when I was growing up. I don't want to hurt his feelings. Now he is sporting a Donald Trumpesque comb over. There are some muffins and a bowl of fruit in the center of the table. I pour myself a glass of OJ and sit down. I regret my drink selection after my first sip. Pulp. I hate pulp. I get back up and grab another glass and experience a blast from the past when I find my mother's mesh strainer on the same hook it hung from when I was in school.

My father watches me, shaking his head as I strain out the pulp. I can still hear him grouching at me all those years ago, trying to convince me the pulp made it healthier. I put my first glass in the dishwasher and go to sit back down, helping myself to a lemon poppy seed muffin and a banana. My dad and I hang out in a comfortable silence. Every time I meet his eyes with mine, he smiles. I'm usually so busy to notice when I'm at work, but sitting here right now, I can't help but wish I lived closer, saw my parents and Brian more often, and any future nieces or nephews. I haven't really talked enough to Brian to see if he and Christine plan to have kids or not. I guess I just assume they will because she's a teacher and therefore I guess likes kids. I hope so. I think Brian would make a good dad, already a good big brother. Well except for befriending the guy who broke his little sister's heart. He kind of sucked ass in that regard.

When my dad finishes his coffee, he rinses his cup and puts it on the counter. He uses the same cup every day. My mom will hand wash it tonight after dinner. Walking past me, he pats me on the shoulder and continues into the living room. He's semi-retired but took this week off for the wedding because I was going to be around. He has always been a man of few words, unlike my mother, who I get my mouth from. Thinking of my mother, I'm excited to see my Uncle

Chip. I had only lived with him for five years in New Jersey before he moved to Florida. He loved Jersey but was over all of the snow in the winter time. He is still my favorite uncle, and I will always owe him one for taking me in like he did. After finishing my breakfast, I go back upstairs to shower and get dressed. I peep out the window when I hear a door slam and race downstairs when I see it's my mom with Chip.

Swinging open the front door, I pull my uncle into a hug. "Nice tan. Florida must be treating you well."

"Hey, kiddo. I'm loving it. Saw you got a shitload of snow last winter. Ready to move yet?"

"You'll be the first to know."

"Alright, you two," my mom says, pushing Chip into the house. "In, in."

I walk backwards into the living room to make room for them. "How was your flight?"

He scrunches his nose, which makes me laugh, and he gives me a confused look. I motion for him to go on.

"I wanted to take a little nap on the plane. I tried the best I could, but Christ, there was this fella somewhere behind me with a god-awful rumble of a snore. I feel bad for whoever sat right around him. Other than that, it was fine. Thank you for asking sweetheart." He tweaks my nose.

"Sarah can you take your uncle's bags up to Brian's old room?"

"I can carry them," he argues, but I grab one anyway and huff it up the stairs. Holy shitcrickets. It's heavy!

I'm gasping by the time I'm at the top. "What's in this?"

Chip shrugs then takes the handle and pulls it the rest of the way to Brian's old room. I head back downstairs and give my mom a good morning kiss on the cheek. She pats my butt, which reminds me how weird my family is.

"Did you eat?" she asks over her shoulder as she walks into the kitchen.

I trail after her. "I did. Where'd you get the muffins?"

"Christine made them. Aren't they great?"

"Shit, she can cook too? How the hell did Brian get her?"

"Language, Sarah."

I smirk. My mother can cuss like a sailor. Chip comes up behind me so I hop on the counter to make room for him to get past. My father comes up behind him, and seeing me on the counter again, throws his hands up. I make a face and slide down off the counter. My mom makes some coffee so I sit with them and have a cup. I can't help but raise an eyebrow at my mother every time she cusses. She looks away like she doesn't see me. They talk about the trouble we used to get into when we were kids, mainly Brian. He was a prankster and always up to something. Luckily, he never did anything really dangerous. It's fun hearing all those old stories. There are a couple I have no memory of.

"Yes, you were there." My mom was adamant.

"Are you sure?" I'm not buying it. I totally would have remembered Brian covering my bedroom door with cling wrap.

She just sits there, nodding while I think about it. Shrugging, I finally give it up. I still can't remember it.

"So what's for lunch?" My stomach is talking, and if I don't get anything in it soon, I will probably eat another muffin.

"Your brother and Christine are bringing subs."

"But how do they know what I want?" I whine.

They all turn to look at me. My mother leans forward and sets her chin in her hand. "Sarah, what is the only sub you have ever ordered since elementary school?"

"Um, a BLT?" I'm not sure why I say it like a question.

"And if you could have any sandwich on the planet today, what kind would you get?"

She doesn't have to look so proud of herself. "A BLT," I grumble.

Chip laughs and pats my upper arm. My mother smiles her world famous 'I know everything why do you even argue with me' smile.

I glance at the microwave to check the time when my stomach rumbles again. "When are they coming?"

"Soon. Eat a banana if you're starving," my mom says, pushing the bowl towards me.

"I had one with breakfast." That's a valid argument, right?

"Heaven forbid you eat two bananas in one day, Sarah."

"Ugh. I don't want another banana, Mom." I push up from the table, about to go upstairs when I hear Brian and Christine walk in the front door. I jog over to them, blowing kisses and taking the food bags.

"Hungry?" Brian's shaking his head.

"Did you have a muffin this morning?" Christine asks, following me into the kitchen.

I'm digging through the bags, looking for my sub as I answer. "Best muffin I've ever had."

"I know, right?" Brian comes up around her and wraps his arms around her waist.

My Uncle Chip stands up to hug and kiss them. I find my sub, and even though it might be slightly rude, I dig in. My mouth is full when Will walks in. I put my hand over my mouth and look towards the back door.

"You didn't wait for me?" He hugs Chip before sitting next to me.

"Only Sarah couldn't wait." My mother smiles at me sweetly as she throws me under the bus.

Now that I've swallowed my bite, I take a deep, soothing breath and reply, "My mother," shooting her a look, "only mentioned Brian and Christine were coming." I look back at her again. "Thanks, mom. Really, thank you."

"It's cool. Brian just thought you might need my help with the slideshow."

I glare at Brian. "What? Why would you think that? I can handle making a slideshow."

"I can go." Will gets up.

Great. Now I'm an asshole. I grab his arm and pull him back down into chair. I refuse to look at him, though, because I may not be able to restrain myself from smacking the smirk I am almost certain is on his face. Instead, I glare at Brian. I'm not sure why it makes me feel better, but it does. It also helps that he looks a bit scared of me. Good. He should be. Chip is giving me a concerned look, I give him a half smile and eat my sub. While we eat, I watch my family interact with Will. I can't lie. It makes me feel jealous that he seems so involved in their lives.

After lunch, Brian, Christine, Will, and I go into the living room to sort through old photos. Christine has brought a bunch of her own that can be used in the slide show. She wants it to start with baby pictures of them and follow them as they grew, ending with pictures of them as a couple. Will brought his laptop and scanner to make the actual file. That bugs me. It seems pretty clear Will can handle making the slideshow on his own. I'm starting to wonder why Brian had even asked for my help. I do my best to put on a happy face, though. I am here for his wedding. There is no way I am going to let my weirdness around Will negatively impact any part of Brian's wedding.

Yes, I am uncomfortable, and yes, I am saying really rude things to both Will and Brian inside my head. All I need to do is be the bigger person for the next week. Besides, no matter how crazy Brian can drive me, he is still my big brother, and I love him. Settling down on the sofa, I reach for a photo album. As I flip through the pictures, I point out cute or funny ones of Brian to Christine. It takes me back. If I had pouted or rebelled against helping because of Will, I might have missed this. I'm still figuring out the whole maturity thing more than halfway through my twenties.

The album I'm looking at has pictures from when Brian was in high school. I don't know why but I hadn't expected to come across pictures of Will and I. When I turn the page, it's like I am pulled back in time. The pictures have to be from our freshman year. There is one with Brian, Will, and I around our kitchen table playing Uno. I have a Yoo-hoo in front of me. I can almost hear Will giving me crap for it, saying they taste like watered down milk. I didn't care. I loved them, still do. I wonder who took the picture, maybe my mom. If my dad had taken it, one of our heads would have been cut off. Thank god for digital cameras. At least my dad could delete the bad shots nowadays. I can't stop looking at the picture. In it, Will and Brian are both smiling straight at the camera. Me, I'm looking at Will like a love sick puppy. It's hard not to remember how intense my feelings for him were.

It takes me a couple seconds to realize everyone has stopped talking. I look up and feel a tear slide down my cheek. I had not even known I was crying. I set the album on the coffee table and hurry into the kitchen. My throat feels dry, so I fill a glass with water and gulp it down. I'm standing at the sink, ready to refill my glass when Will walks in.

"Sarah?"

"Please." It's one word, but the way I say it means so much more. Please don't say anything. Please don't look at me. Please don't hurt me. Please just stay away. Please.

He leans against the doorframe. He never was a good listener. I refill my glass and turn my back to Will before gulping it down. I hear him push off and the sound of his footsteps as he comes to stand right behind me. I can smell his after shave. It's subtle, but intoxicating. When I just barely feel his breath against the back of my neck, I lean onto the counter to ensure I don't fall over. It feels like an eternity. I can't move.

"Can we talk?"

I can't handle this right now. I don't know what to say. Doing nothing, though, seems to work. I hear him swallow before he turns and walks back out of the room. I still can't move. I feel another tear snake down my cheek. I'm not crying because of the picture anymore. Now I'm crying because I know I never stopped loving Will. I'm startled by the noise of the freezer making ice. I turn and almost have a heart attack when I see my uncle Chip sitting at the kitchen table. How the…? I hadn't even heard him come in. My uncle is not a small man. There is no way I could have missing him walking in.

Using his foot, he pushes the chair closest to me out. "Why don't we have a chat, Sarah."

Chapter 10

Past

Our first day back at school is interesting. It feels like the whole school knows about Will kissing me at the amusement park. I have never felt so evaluated. I can only guess what everyone is thinking. What is Will Price doing with her? I don't even have any classes with him to see if he's feeling the same thing. We do have the same lunch, so when the weather's nice we eat outside. I get to our table before him and panic for a moment, wondering if he's changed his mind about me. My fear is short-lived when I see him make his way over to me only moments later. Everyone's eyes follow him as he drops his backpack and leans down to capture my lips. He doesn't break our kiss as he moves to sit next to me. I lean into him and sigh. He pulls back to look at me, tilting his head to the side to smirk at me.

I bump him with my shoulder, and he offers me a French fry. I open my mouth. As I go to take a bite, he pulls it away, eating it instead. He laughs when I pout and nicely feeds me a fry. He looks around us, tensing when he notices everyone has been watching us.

He chews on the corner of his mouth. "How are you doing?"

"It's weird. People never really noticed me before. I wish they'd stop."

He takes my hand in his and kisses it. "I'm sorry."

I reach out to touch his cheek with my other hand. "Don't apologize. You are amazing."

He leans over to kiss my cheek before feeding me another fry.

~*~

At the end of the day, we walk to his car. He opens my door for me before getting in. Once we're out of the parking lot, his hand rests on my thigh as we drive away. My seat is reclined, and I'm on my side, facing him. It's like I don't want to take my eyes off of him. I pull his hoodie from the back seat and use it as a pillow. I glance down to his hand as his thumb slowly strokes my leg. I love the freckle on the back of his hand. Feeling impulsive, I pull his hand to my mouth and kiss it. He looks over at me, giving me a lopsided grin. It's still months away, but I cannot imagine how I will function when he goes to Italy. The language CD is going.

He pulls my hand up to his lips. "Bella ragazza. Wanna go get some ice cream?"

I smile, still not believing William Ethan Price asked me to be his girlfriend. As many times as I had imagined this moment, none of my dreams could hold a candle to what it's like. He kissed me in front of the senior class and again in the cafeteria today. Now he is taking me for ice cream, and he just called me beautiful in Italian. He shakes my knee as he pulls into the parking lot. I pop my seat back up and look for my sunglasses. Will walks around to my side of the car, opening my door and wrapping his arms around my waist once I step out. I put my hands around his neck and run my fingers through his hair.

He rubs his nose against mine. "Why didn't we do this ages ago?"

"You had a girlfriend."

His forehead is pressed to mine. "Why didn't you ever tell me?"

"Tell you what?" I'm confused.

"That you liked me."

"The whole world likes you. I'm kind of trying to figure out why you like me."

"I've liked you for a long time. That's probably why Jessica has been such a bitch. She could totally tell I'd rather be with you."

I don't say anything. I just pull his mouth to mine. He pushes me back, leaning me up against his car.

After a couple moments, he kisses his way up to my ear. "Want to go to my house?"

I pull back, my mouth open. We never go to his house. He hates it over there. Why would he even ask? The idea makes me really nervous, and it's clearly written all over my face.

"My mom is still at work. I thought we could swim in the pool. That way I'm the only one that gets to see you in your bikini."

"Did you still want to get ice cream?"

He gives me a look like, did you really just ask that? Then he kisses me again. The kiss is shorter this time, and holding hands, we walk up together to the parlor. He opens the door for me and comes to stand behind me, his arms around me as we wait to order. There are no other customers in the store, and we both already know what we want. Two scoops of chocolate chip in a chocolate-coated waffle cone for me and one scoop of fudge ripple, one scoop of cherry cordial in a plain waffle cone for Will. We have been coming here together for years and know the owner, Kurt, who is working today.

"You kids finally dating?" he asks, looking at Will's arms around me.

I blush and nod as Will kisses my neck.

"This one is on the house. Think of it as my contribution to young love."

"You don't have to do that, Kurt," Will argues.

"It's my pleasure, kids."

Taking my cone and passing Will his, I turn back to Kurt. "Thank you so much."

It doesn't stop Will from slipping a ten into the tip jar. We walk outside and sit at a small bistro table just to the left of the door. It's like we're afraid to let go of each other. His hand holds mine on top of the table as we eat our ice cream. Will finishes his way before I do, as usual. I'm used to him waiting for me to finish mine, but this time it feels more intense. My hand in his, his eyes watching my mouth and each bite and lick I take. I can't meet his eyes as he watches me. I just flush and look away. A bit of ice cream drips down the side, and I move to catch it. Will's breath hitches as my tongue moves up the side of the cone.

I giggle at his expression, and he groans, turning in his chair to face his car. "I can't watch."

"I'm almost done." I grin.

The idea that I can have a physical effect on him seems impossible to me. I can't help it. I giggle again.

"You know you're killing me."

"I'm sorry." But he knows I'm not.

I finish my cone, and we get up to leave.

Will pulls me to him for another kiss. "Hmm, you taste yummy."

I gasp when he bites my bottom lip. His eyes burn into me when he pulls back. He runs his fingertip down the side of my face before opening my door for me. He drives over to my house so I can change into my suit. He waits in his car, his forehead resting on the top of his steering wheel when I get back in. He leans over to kiss me after I ask if he's okay. When we get to his house, we're quiet. I've only ever been inside a handful of times. It's just not a happy place. When Will was in elementary school, his older sister Bethany died from an undiagnosed heart condition. His mother has never fully moved past that day. Will told me once that nothing in his house has changed since her death. It's like a giant time capsule. I go straight through the kitchen and out to his backyard while Will hurries upstairs to change.

Will is done changing and in the pool before I even have my shoes off. His eyes lock on me as I shimmy out of my shorts and pull my t-shirt off. I make my way over to the stairs and slowly step into the water. Will is waiting for me at the bottom of the stairs. His hands reach out to touch my calves, and with each step I take, they move further up my body. Once his hands touch my waist, I'm lifted and in his arms. He hitches my legs up one at a time until they are wrapped around him. He walks us backwards until we are submerged to our necks.

He takes my mouth, his hands firmly gripping my backside. My hands are in his hair. He's turned on.

I can feel it. It kind of scares me. I don't want to move too fast, but now that I finally have him, I don't want to lose him. I may have tensed. Will pulls back to look at me.

"Are you okay?"

I nod and lower my head to kiss his neck. He moves us out of the deeper water and leans me against the pool wall. The tiles are warmed from the sunny day and hot against my shoulders. I lift my lips from his neck. He grins and lowers his to mine. I lean my head back as he moves his lips lower. His hands have moved up my sides, and his thumbs move back and forth, just barely touching the undersides of my breasts. I'm breathing heavy, my chest rising and falling sharply. His lips dust the swell of my breasts not covered by my top. Conflicted emotions are waging a war inside my head. What do I do if he tries to move my top? Should I let him? God, it feels so good, but I'm nervous.

He moves his lips further up my neck. I lift my head, and his mouth is on mine again. He shifts his hands up, and his thumbs brush across the top of my suit. I shudder in his arms. He lowers his hands and pulls back. I open my eyes, confused. He's chewing on the side of his mouth, his eyes wide. I watch the rise and fall of his chest.

"You shook when I touched you," he said quietly.

I'm not sure what to say. I nod.

He reaches a hand up to cup the side of my face. "You are so beautiful."

"No, you are," I tease.

He's smiling, even though he's shaking his head. "I'm serious. I want to know what you're thinking about all of this."

I blush and look away. "It's all so new." I hesitate. "I get scared."

His thumb brushes my cheek. "Do I scare you?"

"That's not what I meant."

"What did you mean?" I pause. "Sarah, you can say anything to me."

I take a deep breath and look into his eyes "I haven't done all the stuff you have. I'm nervous you'd rather be with someone who has."

His face breaks out into a wide grin. "And I am all knowing?"

"Shut up," I huff.

"Not going to happen. Just think of me as your teacher. Ha! You can call me sir if you want."

"We both know I'm never calling you sir." I turn my face into his palm and bite it. If it's even possible, his eyes widen even more.

"That's why you're the only girl I'll ever want, Miller Lite."

He moves his hand to my waist, pulling us both back towards the stairs in the shallow end. He sits on the middle step. I'm now straddling him. I shift myself off of him, feeling exposed, and sink down to wet my hair. He's leaned back on the stairs, his elbows rested on the next step up. I swim up between his legs and lay my head down on his chest. He brings one hand forward to trail up and down my shoulder blade. I turn my head to kiss his chest. He's lean and cut. I consider licking the ridges of his abs. He surprises me, pushing off the steps, taking me with him. He swings me up into his arms and carries me out of the pool.

He lays down on a lounge, pulling me on top of him. I laugh, propping myself up on my elbows and look down at him. He's grinning, reaching a hand up to push my hair behind my ear. I could look at him all day. He bucks his hips, making me squeal before turning us onto our sides. I rest my head on his shoulder as he kisses the top of it. With his arms around me, we fall asleep.

"What the hell is going on?"

Will tenses next to me, and I blink my eyes open. It's dark out.

"Shit. I guess my mom's home."

I look over my shoulder quickly to see his mom standing in the doorway. She does not look happy. I look up at him, cringing. He leans forward and kisses my forehead. We slowly sit up, and I pull on a tank top and shorts. Stepping into my shoes, I hazard a glance up at Will's mom. I guess I just found out the hard way what the expression 'if looks could kill' feels like. Will has his shirt and shoes on. He grabs my hand and pulls me towards the house.

"I'm going to run Sarah home, mom."

"We are discussing this," she looks at me, "when you get home."

Chapter 11

Present

I lay in bed, trying to find some inner strength to actually go downstairs. Yesterday had pretty much been a disaster, what with embarrassing myself at lunch and then crying over old photos in front of Will. My uncle Chip then proceeded to call me out on all of my bullshit. He knows better than anyone else what I might be going through. He had witnessed it first hand when I showed up a broken-hearted mess on his doorstep all those years ago. No, I never actually told him what had happened that night, but he was smart enough to figure out that it had to do something with Will.

The last thing he had said to me the day before was, "Kiddo, there seems to be some unfinished business between you two. You going to deal with it this time, or are you going to run away again?"

The answer to that question was easy. Run. I talked to Sawyer for a while last night. I wish there was some way I could fly her out for moral support. It's not like she doesn't know my family. Well, everyone but Brian, and seeing as how it is his wedding, I can not think of an excuse. I should have plus one'd from the beginning. She is still certain that I can do this, is even encouraging me to talk to Will. Pretty sure that isn't going to happen. Really, what would be the point? It's ancient history.

I only have four more days to go. My thoughts are interrupted by my stomach. I skipped dinner the night before, and my sub can only hold me over for so long. I glance at the alarm clock. It is just after eight. I check work email on my phone and answer any questions I know off-hand and forward the others to my assistant. I have an out of office auto-reply set up for incoming messages but feel better knowing nothing is blowing up in my absence. When I'm done, I pit stop in the bathroom before heading downstairs. My mom is in the living room reading. She asks if I'm feeling better as I pass. I nod. I had to fake a migraine the night before as an excuse to stay in my room. My dad is at the kitchen table drinking what I assume is his second cup of the day.

He looks up as I walk in. "How's the head?"

"Better." I strain some orange juice and sit down across from him, happy to see there are still a couple of muffins.

I pick at my food, enjoying the quiet. My dad pushes the paper towards me, and smiling at him, I take it and start flipping through it. Out of habit, I go right to the horoscopes. Mine is all mumbo jumbo about Saturn lining up with Venus and investing. I roll my eyes. Will's is less planetary and talks about obstacles to overcome. My dad gets up to pour himself another cup. When he offers me one, I shake my head. My dad has always been so laid back. I wonder how, considering all of the caffeine he ingests on a daily basis. When I'm done with my muffin, I head upstairs to shower, passing Chip on the stairs.

"Hiding under your blanket last night?"

"No comment," I mumble.

Today I am supposed to help my mom wrap ribbons around these sprays of faux flowers that will hang at the end of each pew at the church. After that, I plan to borrow her car and go into town. I have been so busy with work I still need to buy a wedding present. Worst case, if I can't find anything I like on their registry, I can always just write them a check. Once I'm showered and dressed, I head downstairs. My mom has already separated the flowers by color so we can put them together assembly-style. We need to make forty of them.

I pick up a spray of irises. "These match the dresses perfectly."

"Christine looked everywhere for the right color. Once she found these, she bought the whole store out." It was clear my mom was a fan. "Sarah, speaking of your dress. Do you need me to steam it?"

I slap my forehead. "I haven't even taken it out of my bag."

I race upstairs with my mother on my heels. Once in my room, I pull the plastic garment bag it is in from my suitcase. I untie the knot at the bottom and pull the plastic off. My dress is one sky blue wrinkle. I cringe and hold it up so my mom can see it too. She tsks at me as she takes it from me. I don't own many wrinkle-resistant articles of clothing. I follow her to my parents' bedroom and watch as she hangs it in their bathroom.

"Sorry, mom."

She swats my butt as she walks past and tells me not to worry. I follow her back downstairs, and she walks me through how Christine wants the flower sprays to look. By my fourth, I have it down. I look down at the first and second one I made, contemplating taking them apart and redoing them. For each one, we take three pale blue irises, one spray of baby's breath and two green leaves. The irises go in the back, then the leaves and the baby's breath in front. We secure the bundle with a rubber band before twisting pale blue and white ribbons around the stems. Just below the flowers goes a big white ribbon bow. At the church, there are silver rings mounted to the end of each row. The sprays will rest perfectly in the rings.

"Who's making the other floral arrangements?" I ask, picturing Christine and Brian arranging flowers in their apartment.

"They hired a florist for the bouquets, boutonnieres, table toppers, and a couple decorative arrangements for the front of the church. The florist was going to do these sprays too with fresh flowers, but the price was crazy. I told Christine you and I could do it."

"They look great," I say quietly, admiring the finished pile.

"Christine found something on the internet on how to make them."

"Well, if you are ever thinking of a new career," I joke.

My mother has always been crafty. I still have many things she had made over the years, from scarves to jewelry and pottery. For a long time, I tried to talk my mom into selling her stuff at craft fairs or in boutiques. She had zero interest. She just made stuff because it was fun for her, not with any thought of turning a profit. I get that about her but still like to tease her. We are over halfway done when we stop for lunch.

My mom makes a big chef salad with some pita chips on the side. She's trying to keep it light because we have the rehearsal dinner that night. Apparently, it's going to be a hell of a spread, or just hell, considering Will will be there. While I eat my lunch, I blush, thinking of my behavior the day before. I feel so guilty for bailing on the slideshow, especially since Brian had asked me for my help. Lord knows what Will thought of me. Why do I even care what he thought? That internal question may have been the silliest I have ever asked myself. I will always care what Will thinks of me. It is almost part of my DNA at this point.

My mom has a couple of errands she has to run after lunch so I take over the rest of the spray making. Chip hangs out with me. I try, unsuccessfully, to show him how to make one when he offers to help. Flower arranging is not one of his skill sets. Instead, he passes me the next piece I need while I make them. I have loved Chip for as long as I can remember. He seemed larger than life when I was little. He is still tall, but I had caught up to him years ago back in high school. His once dark wavy hair is starting to sport some grey, but it suits him. That is one cruelty in life. Men seem to look distinguished with age. I can only hope I will age as gracefully as my mom and Chip.

He keeps me entertained with all of his exploits in Florida. He has always been a bit of a player. When he speaks, though, I notice something I hadn't before. As happy as he seems to be, part of me wonders if some of that is more for show. Could he be lonely? That isn't something you just come out and ask someone, but the thought troubles me. When I first moved to New Jersey, my uncle Chip had become my hope that I could live alone and be happy, never settling down. If that had changed for him, what would it mean for me?

I am so distracted making the iris sprays I almost forget I still need to get a gift. I borrow my dad's car and go to Crate & Barrel. I'm able to get a list of what Brian and Christine had registered for and what is in stock. Waiting until the last minute means most of the cool things they want have already been purchased. I settle with getting them a side table, assuming it is still on their list because no one wants to pay for shipping. When I look back at the list, I notice they had actually registered for two tables, and someone had already bought one. The table is heavy, though, so I need help getting it to my dad's car. I make my way over to the customer service and almost turn around and leave once I see her. I don't need to see her nametag to know who will be helping me.

"Hi, Jessica."

"Well, I'll be. If it isn't Sarah Miller."

I guess she recognizes me too.

She leans down and sets her chin on her hand. No missing the rock on her ring finger now. "I haven't seen you in forever. In town for a visit?"

I'm not sure I will ever forget the last time I saw her. "My brother is getting married. I actually need help getting a table I'm buying out to my car."

Jessica straightens and presses a button on a Bluetooth-looking thing on her ear. "Carry out assistance needed at service desk," She takes her hand away and looks back at me. "Someone will be up in just a moment. Weddings are the best." She holds out her hand to ensure I see her ring. "I'm getting married in the fall."

"Oh, congratulations."

"Anyone special in your life, Sarah?"

I cringe and shake my head.

"I always thought you and Will would be married by now."

"Excuse me?"

"I always felt..." She tilts her head and changes the subject. "Would you like me to ring you up here?"

"That'd be great. Thanks."

"It's my pleasure."

I see that someone is now behind me, so after paying for the table, I move away from the desk. A high school aged kid with a back brace comes to carry the table out for me. As we exit, Jessica waves at me, smiling, I look at my hand, shocked when I see I'm waving back. I tip the kid a five after he's done loading it and head home. It's hard not to dwell on what Jessica said. After I park, I go and find my dad to ask what I should do about the table. When I explain how heavy it is, he tells me to just leave it in the car. Brian can swing by in the morning with Will and take my dad's car to his place to unload it. My uncle Chip is still hanging out in the living room watching TV. I pick up where I left off and make more sprays.

I am on the last spray when my mom gets back from her errands. She hurries into the room, asking why I haven't started getting ready for dinner. I'm almost offended. How long does she think it will take me to get presentable? I finish the spray and add it to the completed pile. My mother is barking orders at my uncle as I head up the stairs. It's not like I did any heavy labor today, so I don't need to take another shower. I take out my dress, thanking the gods of wrinkle-resistant jersey as I shake it out. It is a charcoal, button-up, shirt-style dress with three quarter sleeves. I do my best to curl my hair the same way Christine had the other night. It doesn't come out as good but still looks pretty when I pull half of it up with a clip. Giving myself a once over after I finish my makeup, I'm happy with how I look.

I turn to check the time. It only took me thirty-five minutes. I consider finding my mother to prove I can clean up nice quickly but don't want to interrupt her. I slip on some black heels, grab my clutch, and go downstairs. My father is straightening his tie in the hall mirror. When he sees me, he whistles.

"Oh, dad," I huff, secretly thrilled. He isn't much of a talker but always seems to know what to say or do to make me feel good.

My uncle Chip comes down the stairs next. We hang out in the living room, waiting for my mother. She takes forever to get ready. She is notorious for changing her mind on what to wear frequently before going out. My dad only checks his watch three more times before she comes down the stairs. I have to grin. She looks beautiful. She wears a shin-length, rose-shaded, sheath-style dress with a floral scarf. She knows she looks good and pauses to let us admire her before coming the rest of the way down the stairs. My father puts his arm out to her, leaning in to whisper something in her ear when she takes it. She blushes and giggles like a schoolgirl.

Ever been so happy for someone and so aware of how lonely their happiness makes you feel at the same time? Chip offers me his arm with a wink, and shrugging, I take it. We may not have dates, but it's a relief to know I will have someone to hang out with tonight. The restaurant we are going to is a bit of a drive, on a local lake. I have a mild panic attack when I realize which lake. Sometimes I feel like I will never be free of that night. I square my shoulders and tell myself to grow up. It was seven years ago. Besides, I am looking forward to meeting Christine's parents and seeing the rest of the wedding party. Well, everyone except Will.

Our group is in a banquet room that opens up on to a deck over the lake. It's a beautiful June evening, and the wide French doors are opened to let in the fresh evening air. I'm curious about mosquitoes but see citronella candle torches lining the deck railing. The flames mirror on the smooth surface of the lake. Chip graciously leads me to my table before joining my parents at the grown ups table. I am not surprised to find myself seated by Will. We are the only single people in the wedding party. Will looks edible, and in some cruel coincidence, I notice his charcoal suit matches my dress perfectly. He brings his hand up to scratch the back of his head. I can not help but flush as I watch his eyes drift over me.

"How are you feeling?" he asks as I slide into my seat.

Oh, the migraine. "Um, better. Thank you." I avoid his eyes.

"I just—"

"Don't."

He doesn't stop. "—wanted to tell you how beautiful I think you look tonight."

I look at my hands in my lap as I spin my ring. "Thank you."

"So what happened the other day?"

Shit. "Nothing."

"Sarah—"

I glare at him, relieved when I see Brian and Christine behind him. "Excuse me," I say getting up.

He grabs my wrist. My mouth drops as I stare at his hand. When he doesn't let go, I look at him. My brows are raised, and he's chewing the corner of his lips. I know what he wants. I can still read his facial expressions. He wants me to let him in. As much as part of me will always want to, I'm smart enough to know how it would all end. I shake my head, and he drops his hand. I hurry towards Brian and Christine, not expecting Will to follow me. I suck in a breath when I feel his hand on the small of my back as he comes to stand next to me.

I try to ignore it. "Brian, Christine, I am so sorry about the other day."

Brian leans into me and kisses my cheek. "Don't worry about it."

Christine pulls me into a hug. "Are you feeling better?"

I nod. "I am, thank you."

Brian looks at Will next to me and gives him a look. Will shrugs. I'm rescued, though, by Christine as she takes my hand to take me around the room to introduce me to her family. Her parents are divorced and both remarried. They seem to get along well enough, and I quickly shake their hands and say hello. Christine's maternal grandmother is also here and wastes no time asking if Will is my boyfriend. When I let her know he is not, she asks Christine for his number. I gape at her until she winks at me, letting me know she's joking, adding she already has a boyfriend. Um, coolest grandma ever. My grandmother on my dad's side is coming for the wedding, but her health is bad so my parents didn't want to stress her out with dinner tonight.

Christine and I head back over to our table. Will and I are seated across from her and Brian. Her maid of honor, Justine, and her husband, Curtis, are seated next to Christine. Another couple, Jacob and his wife, are on the other side of Brian. Roman and his girlfriend, Cindy, are sitting next to me. There is another couple on the other side of Will, but they are doing a reading during the ceremony and had not been out with us the other night, so I don't know what their names are.

Over dinner, Will sits quietly next to me. For a brief moment, I wonder if he is going to leave me alone. Then I feel his leg press against mine. I flinch, dropping my fork. It clangs loudly, and everyone looks at me. I elbow him when I hear him chuckle. I shiver when I feel his breath at my ear.

"I knew you would touch me at some point."

My eyes snap to his. He's leaned back, and his arm is resting across the back of my chair.

"It was my elbow," I hiss.

He shrugs. "Still counts."

"That does not count."

"It does, and now you're talking to me too."

My brows furrow, and I know my face looks like I just sucked on a lemon. I take a deep breath. "I don't understand why you're doing this."

He leans towards me. "Doing what?"

"This," I huff, gesturing between us.

"What? Talking to you?"

I groan and cringe when I see Brian glance at me. He looks concerned. I turn to Will and whisper. "Acting like nothing happened."

His blue eyes pierce me. "I'm not acting like nothing happened."

I scoff, now earning me a glance from Christine.

"Then what are you doing?"

He's chewing on the corner of his bottom lip. He leans back as a server comes around to collect our plates. "I just want you to talk to me."

I roll my eyes. I can't help it. "I'm talking to you right now, Will."

He smirks. "No you're not, you're sitting there, rolling your eyes. You might be hearing the words I'm saying, but we are not talking."

"I seriously don't understand what you're trying to say."

I look up when the slide show starts. The room is quiet when "Chasing Cars" by Snow Patrol starts in the background. That song, with the pictures, I just can't look away. Out of the corner of my eye, I watch Brian wipe a tear from Christine's cheek and give her a chaste kiss on the lips. I become hyperaware of Will next to me. He leans forward, only to pull back again when the dessert dishes come out. He watches me as I stab at my cheesecake. I take a bite, letting it melt on my tongue, trying to block out Will altogether. I just don't know what to do with him, and he doesn't seem capable of telling me. He pushes his plate away and crosses his arms over his chest.

I jump when he suddenly leans towards me again. "Sarah, can we talk outside?"

It's his expression that makes me say yes. I take a sip of my water before I stand, refusing his hand. He gestures for me to go first, coming beside me, his hand again on my back. The heat emanating from his fingertips burns me through my dress. My eyelids flutter as he leads me to a path that winds near the lake. There is a bench. I sit first but move when Will sits too close to me. He stares at the space between us before looking out over the lake. I want to do the same, but I can't seem to tear my eyes from him.

Will leans down and rests his head in his hands. I resist the urge to rub his back. He just seems so, I don't really know, but I know it's making me want to comfort him. He takes a deep breath before he lifts his head to look at me. I can see the light from the restaurant behind us reflected in his eyes.

"The slideshow was beautiful, Will."

He doesn't say anything for the longest time.

"Sarah, why did you leave?"

I close my eyes and shake my head, stopping when I feel his hand cup my cheek. I start to lean into it until I realize what I'm doing and jerk back, my eyes wide. His hand remains suspended in midair for a beat before he lowers it to his leg. I look back towards the lake, crossing my arms over my chest, my hands rubbing warmth into my upper arms. Will shrugs off his jacket, and I lean forward for him to drape over my shoulders. I'm surrounded by his scent. I hazard to look at him and regret it. Why is he doing this? I stand and take a couple of steps forward, needing some distance between us. The gesture is pointless when he follows me.

Fine. He wants to know why I left. I pull off his jacket and thrust it to him. As his hand grips the material, I breathe one word before I take off back to the restaurant. "Jessica."

Chapter 12

Past

I'm so sorry." I've lost count over how many times I've said it. Will's Italian language CD is still on. Piove, it is raining, I hear in the background.

"Sarah, calm down. It was not your fault."

I just can't get the look Will's mom gave me out of my head. "I just feel so bad."

He puts his hand on my leg, making me melt. "I don't."

"I just want your mom to like me."

He squeezes my leg and gives me a lopsided grin.

When we pull up to my house, I expect him to just drop me off. Instead, he parks and follows me inside. "What about your mom?"

He drops a kiss to the back of my neck before reaching into the backseat to grab his camera case. "I'm going to let her stew."

"Will!"

I open the door, and he pulls me towards my bedroom, shutting the door behind him. I kick off my shoes and flop onto my bed, my heart pounding. Will has been in my room hundreds of times, but this time, it feels different. Click. I look up to see him grinning behind his camera. He sets it back in its case on my desk, stepping out of his shoes and coming to stretch out next to me. He's on his side, facing me. His hand moves up to my face to brush some hair behind my ear. I look at him and smile. Will Price is on my bed. I don't want to close my eyes. I'm too afraid that when I wake, it will all be a dream. I move closer to him, and he does the same thing until we meet in the middle of my bed, facing each other. I put my hands on the sides of his face and his arm snakes around my waist. We kiss, his arm pulling me even closer as his tongue teases mine. We are like this when my older brother, Brian, opens the door.

We spring apart as Brian mutters. "You have got to be fucking kidding me."

"Ahhh," is all I can come up with.

"How long has this been going on?" He gestures between the two of us.

Will regains his voice before I do. He reaches out to take my hand. "Not long."

"And you're already making out like that on her bed? Wait, don't you have a girlfriend?" Brian looks like he's going to punch Will.

"They broke up."

"And my little sister is your rebound?"

Will's eyes widen. "She's not a rebound. I broke up with Jessica for her."

He did? I smile at him, and he sweeps his thumb across the back of my hand.

"Sarah, go to my room. I want to talk to Will alone." Brian pops his knuckles.

Oh shit. "What? No way. Anything you want to say to Will you can say in front of me."

Will squeezes my hand. "It's okay, Sarah."

Brian motions towards his room with his head.

"Fine," I grumble, squeezing Will's hand one more time before I let go.

Brian shuts my door behind me. I walk into his room and sit on his bed. The fact that I know they are talking about me but I don't know what either of them are saying is driving me crazy. I nervously spin my ring until Brian opens the door, and Will walks out into the hallway.

I jump off Brian's bed and run over to him "What'd he say?"

Brian looks back and forth between us. "What I said was for Will's ears only, but here's something for the both of you. No more hanging out in your room together, period. Get your asses down to the family room before I tell mom and dad what I saw you two doing."

"Brian," I whine.

He shakes his head and points down the stairs.

"I need to grab my camera," Will explains, stepping back into my room. Brian waits, watching him until he's back out of my room. Taking Will's hand, I slowly walk down the stairs and tug him towards the family room.

He stops me. "I should probably head home."

I glare up at Brian, who shrugs and walks into his bedroom.

"Are you sure?"

"You heard my mom. Walk me out?"

I nod and walk out barefoot. Will must have put his shoes back on after Brian was done talking to him. We walk out to his car. He puts his camera case on the floor of the backseat and shuts the door. He leans his back against his door and pulls me to his chest, wrapping his arms around my waist.

"What did Brian say to you?" I ask, resting my cheek on his chest, smiling as I listen to his heart beat.

He lifts my chin so I'm looking up at him. "Nothing any good big brother wouldn't say."

He dips his head and presses his lips to mine. I rest my arms on his shoulders and run my fingers through his hair.

He breaks our kiss and rests his forehead on mine. "You know you're not a rebound, right?"

I didn’t, but I don’t doubt the sincerity of his question so I nod my head. He lifts me off the ground and kisses me again. I don’t want him to leave, but after a few moments, he sets me back down and does.

"Call me after you talk to your mom," I yell as he's backing away.

I will, he mouths.

I hurry back inside and race up to Brian's room, flinging his door open. "What did you say to Will?"

Brian is lying on his bed, his telephone to his ear. "Hey, let me go," he says before hanging up. I walk over and sit on the edge of his bed.

He sits up and leans against his headboard, his brown hair flopping into his eyes. "Look, I only told him that I'll kill him and no one will ever find the body if he hurts you."

"Brian," I gasp. "I cannot believe you did that. What if you've scared him away?"

He laughs at me. "Sarah, that boy has been in love with you for years."

"No, he hasn’t." I wrinkle my nose at him. "Um, everyone at our school likes him. He's wonderful."

"I don’t know why he waited this long, but it's the truth."

"You're crazy, and if you scared him away, I'll never forgive you."

Brian moves closer to me and puts his arm around my shoulders. "Nothing is going to scare that boy away from you." He kisses my temple before laying back down. "Now get out and shut the door behind you. I'm trying to iron out my Friday night over here," he says, picking his phone back up.

I shut his door a bit harder than necessary and go into my room, checking my phone to make sure Will hasn't called yet. What a day. With the exception of Will's mom finding us asleep together on a deck chair and Brian threatening bodily harm on him, it was the best day of my entire life. I change for bed and go wash my face and brush my teeth, checking my phone again when I'm back in my room. Still no call. I do the math in my head. It takes fifteen minutes to get from my house to his, and he left an hour ago. Does that mean he's been talking to his mom for the last forty-five minutes? I wonder if she told his dad. Are they both talking to him? What if they forbid him from seeing me again?

The not knowing is killing me. I grab my phone and text him.

Everything ok?

I hold my phone in front of my face like a crazy person, willing him to reply. Five minutes go by. I climb into bed and prop my phone up on a pillow in front of my face. I'm hungry. We had skipped dinner, but I ignore it. I stare at my phone so long I fall asleep, jerking when he calls me.

"Will?"

"Hey."

He sounds tired. "What'd your mom say?"

"Don't worry about her. She was just not expecting to come home to that. I think she was more weirded out by me having someone over than us being asleep."

"Are you sure?"

"Cross my heart."

I hear him yawn. "Did you want to talk more tomorrow?"

"No, I'm good. I don't want to hang up."

I laugh. "You sound like you're about to fall asleep."

"'M not," he mumbles before yawning again.

His yawns are contagious, and I yawn. "You're making me sleepy."

"I wish I was there."

That makes me pout. "I wish you were too."

"Will you go with me to prom?"

"Really?"

There is a long pause. "Will?" I wonder if he's fallen asleep.

"I'm here."

"Did you hear what I asked?"

"I did. I was just thinking of a way to say what I wanted to say without it seeming lame."

"Lame? Just spit it out."

"I want everyone to see you're with me."

I snort. "I'm pretty sure they all know that."

"I get that they see us kiss, but I want everyone to know you're my girlfriend."

I don’t get it. "Will, everyone knows it. Is there something else?"

"Aren't girls supposed to be all about prom? I just want to make you happy."

"I don't really care about prom. All I want is you, Will."

"I'm all yours. I'd like to go only if you want to."

Hearing him say that makes me melt. "Oh, Will. Of course I'll go to prom with you."

Our phone conversation goes on between yawns for another fifteen minutes. After a ‘no, you hang up first’ battle, I finally hang up and fall asleep.

Chapter 13

Present

Brian gives me a strange look as I return to my seat. I smile brightly and look away, blinking back tears that are threatening to spill. Why had I even gone outside with him? That was a stupid mistake, and I need to be more careful. It is taking everything not to pull out my cell phone and purchase a seat on the next flight out of here. As much as I want to escape and put as many miles as I can between myself and these painful memories, I cannot hurt my brother like that. It means so much to him that I came, and after meeting Christine, I was glad that I had, even if other stuff hurt.

It strikes me as odd, though that in all the times Brian or my mother and I had talked over the years, neither of them had ever brought Will up. He seems pretty ensconced in their lives. Did they hide his involvement on purpose? I need to relax, I just sit there, nervously waiting for Will to come back inside and sit back down. I'm so distracted I jump when my uncle Chip lowers himself into Will's seat instead.

"Hey, Bri. Will had to take off. He wasn't feeling well." Chip glances at me. "He wanted me to let you know."

He left because of me. I know it. I feel awful until I remember this is my brother's wedding. If someone should leave, it should be him, but I still feel bad. There are times I hate Will, for what had happened and for what he had done. I lost a piece of myself that night, and in all of these years, have never found it. That night changed me. I was so naïve and trusting and mostly in love. I am no longer naïve, and I cannot say with certainty I trust anyone other than myself. Love, that one I'm stuck with. As much as I hate Will sometimes, I will always love him. Sometimes, still caring for him that way is what hurts the most.

After the reception, I ride back with Brian and Christine to their place. Brian wants to show off their condo, and I'm curious to see him living like a grown up. Their building is small, and their place is on the third floor. They have one assigned spot that Christine's car is already in, so parking is interesting given the time of night. Brian lucks out, catching a spot close to the building when someone leaves. They hold hands as I follow behind, envying the gesture. Christine turns back to point out things as we walk up.

There is no elevator. Halfway up the stairs, I think about taking my shoes off, but I'd be barefoot, so gross.

When we reached their door, I compliment the wicker wreath they have hanging on it. Something makes me guess it's Christine's. The door opens into a little foyer. To the right, there's an open concept living room, dining room, and a guest bedroom they use as an office, and to the left is the kitchen and master bedroom. Straight ahead are two closets and a full bath. In the middle of the foyer sits a small round wooden table with irises.

"Must be your favorite." I gesture towards them, thinking of the sprays I assembled.

Christine beams. "Yes, my absolute favorite. What's your favorite flower?"

I hesitate. Only one other person knows the answer to that question. "Lilies."

I step out of my shoes, relishing the relief that comes with being barefoot after spending too much time in heels. Brian heads into the kitchen to make us drinks while Christine and I go to their living room. She sits on their sofa while I look around. The ceilings seem taller than both my parents' place and my place in Denver. It makes the space feel bigger than it actually is. There are framed pictures everywhere, mainly of the two of them and a few with friends. I pause to look at one of Brian and Will. It still bothers me that I had not known how close they became after I left. There are other black and white prints that catch my eye. All shadow and light across structured objects, fence posts, deck planks, back slats of a chair. They're beautiful.

"Will took those," Christine murmurs from the sofa.

I close my eyes, shutting them out before turning and giving her a noncommittal smile.

Brian walks in with our drinks and sits down next to Christine. I take mine and sit across from them in a rounded armchair. It hugs me. I sink deeper into it, bringing my legs up and curled them to my side.

"This is a great place, guys." I look at my brother. "Brian, before I forget, I picked up your wedding present today. Not to ruin the surprise, but it's a heavy ass table and in the back of dad's car. He said maybe you and Will could swing by in the morning to pick it up while we're getting our salon on." I smile at Christine and she raises her glass.

Brian grins and looks at Christine, "So is it a dark wood end table with geometric cut out carvings on the sides?"

Why does he look so happy? "Yeah, so?"

"Will got us the other one."

I roll my eyes and shake my head. Of course he did. Probably even chatted Jessica up when he was there.

"Oh my gosh," Christine gushes. "It's like you two are a matched set!"

Did she really just say that? "Well, that was fun. Let's talk about something else now. Please."

Brian smiles. "Anything you want, sis. I'm thrilled you like the place. When you have a sec, go check out the kitchen. We have a balcony off of it, and our bedroom overlooks the center courtyard."

I take a sip of my drink and close my eyes. "Geez, Brian. If you're drinking what I'm drinking, are you sure you'll be able to drive me home?"

He shrugs. "I can always have Will come pick you up."

"Not cool," I blurt, not thinking.

Brian leans forward. "Seriously, what is the deal between you two?"

I look away. "Long story," and take another drink.

"Come on, Sarah. We have all night."

I give him a look. "No, you don't. You're getting married tomorrow. A good night of sleep is probably in your best interest. Speaking of, are you all even supposed to be sleeping together the night before the wedding?"

"Nice dodge." He puts his arm around Christine. "I'd like to see someone tell me to stay away. So, you, Will. What's the deal?"

"Brian, leave her alone. If Sarah wanted to talk about it, she would."

I raise my glass to her. I'm liking this girl better every minute. Besides, short of booking a flight out of here, my next plan of attack is to not exhume buried skeletons. Seems safer that way. When we finish our drinks, Christine shows me the rest of their place. Their kitchen is galley-styled with an old-fashioned farmhouse table island. There are Adirondack chairs and a bistro table on their balcony. I lean against the railing and look at the courtyard below. Christine comes to stand beside me.

"Will used to live in that one," she says, pointing to a condo across the courtyard. "When he lived there, he and Brian would try and throw a football back and forth." She shakes her head. "Never worked. One of them would always have to run down to get the ball." She pauses. "Did you hear about Will's dad?"

I nod. "Will told me."

"His mom is not taking it well, which I can understand. He's a good guy to take care of her."

"Did you know about his sister?"

Christine shakes her head. "He had an older sister who died when he was in elementary school. It was something to do with her heart."

"That's awful. I didn't know."

"Growing up, I remember he never wanted to be at his house. It made him uncomfortable" I close my eyes, kicking myself for even mentioning it.

Brian comes out. "I should probably get you back home before it gets too late."

I hug Christine and compliment her again on their place. It feels good to see my brother settled. I slip my shoes back on and take Brian's arm when he offers it. I lean into him, feeling guilty it has been so long since the last time I saw him. He takes Sarah's car so he won't have to hunt for a spot when he gets back, opening the door for me.

On the way to our parents' house, he starts again. "Why can't you tell me what happened with Will?"

I shrug. "It hurts too much."

It's the truth, and it shuts him up until we reach our neighborhood.

"For what it's worth, he's hurting too."

I shake my head, suddenly angry. "He doesn't get to hurt."

"Shit, Sarah. When you say stuff like that, it makes me feel like I should kick his ass."

He parks in front of the house. "Then it's probably best that you don't know."

Chapter 14

Past

"Brian, please," I beg.

He looks up at the ceiling "Don't you have a girl who can help you with this?" He must see my expression fall because he quickly adds, "Sure, I'll help you."

I throw my arms around him. "Thank you, thank you, thank you."

He pats my back. "Just know Will probably won't like the dress I pick out for you. I'm thinking something ankle-length with a built in hoodie."

I pull back and glare at him. "Brian, be serious."

"Fine, go get your purse. We can go now."

I run upstairs to grab my purse. He's waiting for me in his car. He turns off the radio the second I have my seatbelt on. Brian is usually all about his tunes. I turn and look at him. He looks nervous.

"Everything okay?"

He pushes out a breath of air. "I'm actually happy we have this chance to hang out tonight. I know you and Will are getting serious, and I wanted to talk to you about that."

I blush. He isn't. He wouldn't. Oh my God, I think he's going to try and talk to me about sex. "Brian..."

"I know you probably don't want to talk about this. Trust me. This is the last thing I want to talk to you about, but you're my baby sister, and I have to know. Have you and Will, well, you know?"

"No!"

He exhales. "Are you going to? Prom?"

I spin my ring and look out the window. "This is so embarrassing."

"You don't think this is embarrassing me?"

I glance over at him and have to hold back a laugh. He's sweating. "I just, I don't know. Don't be mad."

He head whips towards mine. "Mad? Why would I be mad?"

"Ugh, Brian! You are not making this easy."

"Fine. Shutting up. Please continue."

"Will doesn't want to rush me..."

"Otherwise, I'd kill him."

"Brian!"

"Right, shutting up."

"I think I want to, you know, do it." I wait for him to say something. "Brian?"

He holds up a finger so I wait, in silence, in his car, after just telling my big brother I want to have sex with my boyfriend.

It feels like forever before he replies. "I think you should go on the pill."

"Will you help me?"

"Dude, you even notice we're not headed to the mall anymore?"

I look around and realize I have no clue where we are. "Where are we going?"

"Free clinic. You're getting on the pill."

"Brian, how do you know where the free clinic is?"

He shrugs. "Not my first rodeo."

"Eww."

He just laughs and pulls into the parking lot of a small brown building.

"Are you going to come in with me?"

"Sure."

After I'm signed in, we wait thirty minutes before the physician is able to see me. Brian waits for me in the waiting room during my exam. My doctor is a woman. I think I would have been so embarrassed if it was a guy. She talks to me about STDs and how my pills will not protect against them and to use a condom as well. She puts some in a bag with my pills. She also explains when I should start taking the pills and how long I need to be taking them before they're effective. Brian stands up and walks over to me as soon as I walk back into the waiting room. I giggle when I realize the staff probably thinks he's my boyfriend. Gross.

"You okay?" he asks.

"Let's just get out of here."

Once we're in his car, he turns and asks again.

"I am. Thanks for taking me. It was just weird."

"I love you, Sarah, and I really don't want to be an uncle anytime soon."

I punch his arm. "I love you too."

"Still feel like," he takes a deep breath, "dress shopping?"

I grin and nod.

He rolls his eyes and heads towards the mall.

~*~

"So what color is your dress?"

I close my locker. "Not telling you."

He grabs my hand. "I just need to know what color corsage to get you."

"Oh, I thought you—never mind. It's black."

He chews the corner of his mouth. "Do they have black flowers?"

I laugh and stand on my tip toes to kiss him. "Black goes with anything, silly. We can pick whatever color we want."

He holds the door open for me as we walk out to the parking lot. "So what color corsage do you want?"

I cringe. "I don’t know. White or red. What do you think?"

He slips my backpack off my shoulder and tosses it with his into the backseat of his car. Closing the door, he leans me up against his car, pressing his hips against mine. "Anything you want," he whispers in my ear as he kisses my neck.

"I want you."

He lifts his head and looks in my eyes "I'm sorry. I missed that."

I blush but hold his gaze. "I want you."

He dips his head to kiss me. "You got me, Miller Lite."

"Will," I sigh.

His brows come together. "What?"

We turn our heads when someone shouts hello across the parking for us get a room. Will kisses me again and reaches behind me to open my door for me. When we're both in his car, he turns to me and asks if I'm okay.

I look down at my ring and spin it before I look up at him. "Do you want to, you know, have sex with me?"

His eyes widen. "Of course, but I don’t want you to feel rushed."

"I don't," I watch as he closes his eyes, "want to wait."

His eyes pop open and snap to mine.

I say it again. "I don't want to wait."

His mouth is on mine, his fingers threaded through my hair. A tap on the driver's side window brings us back to earth. Our school's track coach motions for us to hit the road. Will nods, adjusting his shorts before he starts his car.

Once we're on the main road going towards my house, Will speaks. "Are you sure?"

Yes. We've only been dating for just over a month, but it's Will. There is no other person on the planet I would trust more for my first time. Besides, how many people can say they lost their virginity to someone they had been in love with for over six years?

"I love you.."

He takes my hand and kisses my knuckles while he drives. "I love you so much, Sarah Miller, so much."

I exhale and unsuccessfully try to blink back tears as I sniffle. Will, my Will, just told me he loves me. I feel this pressure within my chest as though it's expanding with emotion I am unable to contain. Will tightly grips my hand as he keeps glancing over at me with a concerned expression on his face. He relaxes once he's parked in front of my house.

He kisses my hand once more before releasing it to cup my face. He studies me. "Please say something."

"I just can't believe you love me too." I croak, my eyes brimming.

All of the tension drains from his face as the corners of his mouth pull up into his lopsided grin. "Believe it," he murmurs, his lips hovering above mine.

"Kiss m—"

His mouth crushes mine before I finish my command. I lift my hands to tangle in his hair. I moan when his teeth nip at my bottom lip. If we weren't in front of my house I probably would have crawled into his lap. He breaks our kiss and looks up at the ceiling of his car as he catches his breath. I'm doing the same, only watching his chest rise and fall as he inhales and pushes the air back out.

He turns to look at me after a couple moments. "So much."

I nod. "Me too."

"Can I take your picture?"

I cover my face. "I must look awful. My eyes are probably red, and my nose—"

He cuts me off. "You're the most beautiful girl I've ever seen."

His words destroy any argument I have. I only ask that he take one of the both of us as well. He reaches into the backseat and fishes it out of its case.

"Tell me you love me again."

"I love you, Will."

I hear it click three times during. He lowers his camera and leans forward to place his lips on mine. "Thank you."

He turns the camera and holds it out to face us, his finger ready. I lean in and kiss his cheek when I hear the click. He turns his face to kiss me, and I hear the click again.

He pulls back and smiles. "Hopefully we'll be in that last one."

He reaches back to place his camera back in its case. I get out and wait for him to walk around. He pulls our bags from the back seat, passing me mine before we head into my house. Before Brian caught us making out on my bed, we would sometimes do our homework in my room. Since then, we stay in the family room. That doesn't stop us from making out. It just makes us hyper aware of where my family members are. Brian is back at school. He comes home at least one weekend a month, but during the week, we don't have to worry about him. Both my mom and dad work, so right after school we usually have the house to ourselves. The family room is far enough from the front door that if one of my parents comes home earlier than expected we have enough time to separate and adjust clothes.

Today, we can't keep our hands off of each other. We take a moment to spread a couple of text books and binders on the coffee table to make it look like we've been busy with schoolwork before Will pulls me on to the couch. We've made out before, even done some under clothes exploring but with our declarations of love so fresh on our lips, this time feels different. Will's shirt is off, and my button-up top is open. My bra has a front closure. Will stills when I unclasp it. I don't uncover myself. I just lay there, holding my breath. Will's own breathing is unsteady as he holds my gaze, lifting his hands to uncover me. His touch is tender as he trails his fingertips across my skin.

"You are so beautiful," he says in a hush tone before dropping his lips to mine.

I wrap my arms around his neck and deepen his kiss. He lowers his body onto mine, and I feel for the first time the perfection that is his bare chest on mine. I grip his shoulders as his hips grind into me. He's turned on. Part of me wants to go all the way right now, but my parents could come home anytime. He moves onto his side, pulling me with him and unbuttons my shorts. His lips stay on mine as his hand makes its way into them. This is the farthest we have ever gone. I tense as I feel him touch me. The feeling, taking over me, scares me. A small part of me wants to stop, but it's only because I'm afraid of the unknown. I suck in a breath and close my eyes when I feel his finger slide inside me. When he starts moving it, my eyes flutter open and widen as he watches my reaction. I want to bury my face in his neck.

"Don't," he pleads. "Let me watch you."

I blush but hold his gaze, even when I lose control and rock against his hand. I've never felt anything like this before. I feel like my limbs are numb and weighted down. It's a few moments before I can breathe normally again. The whole time, his face is a picture of awe. He seems surprised he has this power over my body. He helps fix my clothes before pulling his shirt back on. I start towards the kitchen to get us drinks, turning back when he calls out my name.

"Wear a dress tomorrow."

I look at him confused. "Why?"

He grins. "I want to try something different." He pauses, chewing the corner of his mouth. "You'll just have to wait and see what."

I start to sag and reach my arm out to brace myself on the doorway. His chuckle follows me into the kitchen. We're innocently working on homework when my mother gets home. She invites Will to stay for dinner, and I'm surprised when he declines. After he puts his books back in his bag, I walk him out to his car.

"I wish you would stay."

He puts his bag in the backseat before tugging me into his arms. "I promised my dad I'd be home for dinner tonight."

"Oh." I try not to sound disappointed.

He cups my face and brushes his lips across mine. "Call you after?"

I nod and rest his hands on his waist.

He rests his forehead against mine. "I love you so much."

"I love you too, Will."

He kisses me again, and I pull back to watch him get in his car and pull away. Once he turns off my street, I walk back into my house. My mom asks me to set the table. My dad gets home just as I finish. It's probably a good thing Will isn't here tonight. It gives me a chance to ask my parents about my curfew for prom. When Brian was a senior, he got to stay out all night. It's only fair that they let me.

My dad disagrees. "Brian didn't have a girlfriend, Sarah."

"But, Dad, that's almost worse. Don't you guys trust me not to do anything stupid?"

"Of course..."

"Well, why is it different for me then? Is this because I'm a girl? That's so not fair."

"Honey." My mom puts her hand on my arm. "Let your father and I think about it, and we'll let you know."

I relax. That means she's on my side. I avoid my dad's eyes because I don't want him to get annoyed. As soon as I'm done eating, I excuse myself and hurry up to my room. I'm finishing my math homework when my mom peeks her head in the doorway.

"I talked to your father."

"And?"

"No curfew, but I wanted to talk to you first."

"About what?"

"Are you and Will…?"

"Mom!"

"Honey, don't be embarrassed. I just want to know if you are being safe."

"We haven't done anything, Mom."

She exhales. "Alright, well if you do."

"I will, Mom. I promise."

She walks over and kisses my forehead. "I can't believe how grown up you've gotten."

My phone starts ringing. "It's Will," I say.

She nods her head and walks out of my room, closing my door behind her.

"Hey, how was your dinner?"

"Good. My dad just said he never saw me anymore."

"Oh, That's cool. I talked to my parents about prom."

"What'd they say?"

"I'm yours all night." I smile.

"I'm pretty sure they didn't say that," he jokes.

"You know what I mean."

"I do. So since I'll have you," he pauses, "all night. What do you want to do?"

"Maybe we could, um, get a room somewhere."

"You don't want to go to any after parties or anything?"

I hesitate. "Do you?"

"No, but I'll do anything you want."

I pull one of my pillows to my chest and hug it, wishing it was him. "I only want you."

"You and me, all night?"

"Mm hmm."

"Let's go out to dinner tomorrow night?"

"What?" I laugh. "Why?"

"You're my girlfriend. Let me take you out, please."

"We're together every night already. You don't have to take me anywhere."

"I want to. Come on. I'll show you a good time."

I'm glad he isn't there to see me blush. "Alright, what time are you picking me up?"

~*~

Will drops me off instead of coming in after school. I want to surprise him for our date. There's a dress my mom got me last year that I've never been brave enough to wear. It isn't fancy. It's just tighter than the stuff I usually wear. I take my time getting ready and borrow a pair of heels from my mom. My dad's mouth drops when he sees my dress. He starts to say something but my mom shushes him, telling me I look beautiful. I gulp when I hear the doorbell. I can't even remember the last time Will didn't just walk right into my house.

My mom tells me to wait while she goes to let him in. When I see him, I have to tell myself not to drool. He's just so handsome. His expression when he sees me makes me melt. When my mom and dad are looking away, he mouths wow to me, his eyes lighting up. My mom embarrasses me by taking a picture of us. From this angle, my parents can't see his hand slide down my back and over my ass. I almost laugh at how serene his face looks for the picture, considering where his hand is. Once we're outside, he looks behind us to see if my parents are watching before crushing my body to his.

"Damn, Sarah. Wow. You look incredible."

"You look pretty good yourself," I grin.

And he does in his tan slacks and blue button-up dress shirt. The blue matches his eyes, amplifying them. He walks around to open my door, waiting until I'm buckled to close it. As we drive, his hand is glued to my knee. It's silly, but I'm so excited about our date, our first official one. He takes me to a Mexican place with the best salsa. Once we're seated, we dig in until the server comes to take our orders.

"Brian took me to get on the pill," I blurt out.

Will freezes, chip midair. After a moment, he sets the chip back into the salsa. "For real?"

I nod.

He looks at the people eating around us before leaning towards me. "Does that mean..?"

I shake my head. "Not by prom, but after."

"Would you want to?"

My brows come together. "I thought we were going to..."

"No, I meant," he pauses, "without a condom."

"Oh," I spin my ring."Have you ever..?"

He shakes his head.

"Would you want to?"

"Only if you do."

I unroll the napkin and lay it across my lap. We both look up when the server comes. After he leaves, Will reaches his hand across the booth for mine. Once my hand is in his, he rubs his thumb back and forth across the back of it.

"I don't know, maybe."

He nods, lifting my hand in his to kiss it.

"Anything you want."

"Can I ask you something?"

"Of course."

"What's it like? You know...sex."

He cringes and clears his throat. "I'm not sure for a girl."

"How many people have you done it with?" This was something we never talked about before.

He chews the side of his lip. "One."

I cringe. "Jessica?"

He looks down and nods. I don't know why it bothers me, but the thought of them together kills me.

"And she wasn't a virgin?"

He shakes his head. "She dated this guy, Brice, for two years before his family moved to Maine."

I hadn't known that. "A lot?"

He shakes his head. He lets go of my hand when our food comes out. We eat quietly, and I start to feel bad for bringing it up. I just wanted to know, but now that I do, I wish I didn't. I relax when Will asks if I'd like to go for ice cream after.

Once we're in his car, he asks if I'm okay.

"I hate thinking about you and Jessica being together," I admit.

"I shouldn't have done it. I guess I was excited I could, but I didn't love her. I know the difference now."

When he opens my door for me, I know I'm over it. Jessica doesn't matter. Will loves me, and that's all I need.

Chapter 15

Present

My mom and I are meeting Christine and the rest of the bridal party at a local salon for our hair and makeup. I'm having a hard time forgetting the look on Will's face when I told him why I left. That, more than anything else, gets me out of bed. I need to be busy, distracted. I check work emails on my phone and am relieved to see everything seems to be going smoothly. I take my shower before heading downstairs. There is no point doing anything more than getting dressed since everything else will be taken care of at the salon. I change into jeans and my bridal party t-shirt. It's a personalized pale blue one that says Mr. & Mrs., 6-20-2013 on the front in thick, white shimmery script, and then on the back it says Sarah, bridesmaid, sister of the groom in the same script. I have to give it to Christine. Not only is she crazy organized, but the t-shirts are useful and cute. Once we're at the salon, all the stylists will need to do is check the back of our shirts to know who we are.

Both my mother and father are in the kitchen when I come down. My mom is too cute in her bridal party t-shirt. No multiple outfit changes this time, I think to myself. I kiss my dad on the cheek and blow one to my mom before I go to strain my orange juice. My mom starts to get up to help, but I wave her off. I'm bummed to see we are out of muffins when I sit down at the table. My dad looks a bit guilty and looks away. I bet he ate the last one. I make do with a slice of my mother's cranberry date bread. She usually only makes it around Christmas time, but it's my uncle Chip's favorite so she made some just for him.

When I'm done eating, I help my mom lay our dresses across her backseat before running back inside to grab a bag of extra stuff I'll need to get ready. The ladies will finish getting ready at Christine's mom's house, the guys at my parents' house. There are three hair stylists and one makeup artist for our group. I hang out with my mom as she gets her makeup done. Christine's mom comes over to us with mimosas. We grin at each other and each take one. I'm on my third by the time I'm getting my hair done when Christine's mom offers me another one. I decline, asking for a water instead. This could be a very interesting wedding if we are all drunk before noon.

My long brown hair is curled and twisted into a complicated-looking up do with crystal tipped pins weaved throughout. I hold my breath and close my eyes as the stylist puts a ridiculous amount of hairspray on it. My brow creases as I wonder how long it will take to wash out tomorrow. I drink some water and go to sit and wait to have my makeup done. When it's my turn, I close my eyes and relax as Kim, the artist, chats and works her magic. She goes on about primer and how important it is to use as a base, but primer just makes me think of paint.

She has me open my eyes when it's time for my mascara. I blink at my reflection in the mirror. Kim is a genius. I am not sure if I have ever looked like this. She clears her throat, raising the wand in her hand to get my attention. I apologize and try not to blink as she coats my lashes. When I'm all done, I make my way to the ladies' room before looking for my mom. She is with Christine. When she sees me, her eyes light up. Christine, whose back is to me, follows her gaze and turns around.

"Wow. Will is not going to know what hit him."

"Will?"

Christine's smile falters as she takes in my expression. "Never mind."

I move around to sit next to my mom, facing her. "Tell me."

Her eyes flick to my mom's before looking back at me. I turn to my mom, who picks up her mimosa and takes a sip in an effort to avoid mine.

"Seriously. You too?"

She stares at a poster on the wall of a model with an angled bob. "I'm not sure what you mean."

I lean back, folding my arms across my chest and look at Christine. "Tell me."

She seems to consider it for a moment before leaning forward. "Will is in love with you."

"Christine!" my mother exclaims.

"What?" She shrugs. "Sarah has to know."

They both look at me. I'm just shaking my head. "That's just not true."

"Sarah—" my mother starts, but I stand and hurry out the front door.

I pace back and forth in front of the salon. Why would Christine say that? Does he regret what happened? I told him why I left the night before, and he had made no move to correct me. I move over to a shaded spot of the parking lot and sit on the curb. I'm still sitting there when everyone comes out. My mother and I ride in silence to Christine's mom's house. I carry my dress and bag and am directed to a spare bedroom to change. I manage to get my dress on all by myself. I just need someone to close the very last clasp at the top of the zipper. I reapply my deodorant before putting everything I had on before in my bag and slip on my shoes. I'm in search of someone to help with the clasp when I pass a tall mirror in the hall. My mother did a wonderful job removing any creases. The bridesmaid dresses are tea-length with a halter-styled neck and a poofy skirt.

Justine and Cindy walk out of a room further down the hall and motion for me to join them.

"That color is so good on you, Sarah," Cindy gushes. "I look so washed out."

I look at her. She is crazy. It looks great on her, and I tell her as much before following them to go see Christine in her dress. My mother, her mother, and her step-mother are helping her in the master bedroom. We oh and ah over her as soon as we see her. Her mother and my mother are both dabbing their eyes with tissue. Her dress is strapless with a full, elaborately beaded skirt and train. I can't help but think my brother is one lucky guy. Christine calls us over and gives each of us a personalized jewelry box with a matching crystal necklace and earrings as another bridesmaid gift. They match the set she is wearing and the pins in our hair. She has to be the most organized person I have ever met.

I've just had my mother attach my clasp when a knock at the front door alerts us that the limo has arrived. I help my mother put our bags in her car. The moms are all riding with her over to the church, Christine and us bridesmaids following in the limo. It is a group effort getting Christine into the limo with her full skirt. We are taken around the back of the church and told to wait while my mom gets out bouquets from the florist. Christine is radiant, happy, maybe a little nervous, but ready. We apply last minute lip gloss and giggle while we wait for my mom. I go to open the door when we hear a knock. Expecting my mom, I gasp and slam the door in his face when I see Brian.

"Who is it?" Christine asks, looking at my surprised expression.

"Brian," I blurt, and her mouth drops.

"Is everything okay?" she asks.

"I didn't ask," I admit.

I stand next to her as she cracks the door, careful to stay behind it. "Brian? What are you doing?"

"I just wanted to see you." He's just on the other side of the door.

"That's bad luck." She moves further behind the door.

"I mean talk to you," he corrects. "Can I hold your hand?"

She smiles and slips her hand through the opening.

"Chris, I just couldn't wait to tell you how much I love you and how you are making me the happiest man on earth by marrying me today. I just want you to know that every day for the rest of our lives, I'm going to do everything I can to make you as happy." He lifts her arm and kisses her hand.

Christine looks like she's going to cry. "You already make me so happy. I love you so much, Brian."

He kisses her hand again and tells her he'll be the guy at the alter before leaving. I can hear my mother fuss at him as he walks away. I open the door to help my mom as Christine's bridesmaids gush over how romantic my brother is. I have to hand it to him. That was one of the most beautiful moments I have ever witnessed. It takes Christine a moment to come back to earth. She has a dreamy look on her face as I hand her the bouquet. Her father comes to get us not long after to let us know everyone is seated. The son and daughter of Justine and Curtis serve as flower girl and ring bearer. Caitlin is only two so Braden, her big brother, pulls her in a small decorated wagon as she throws pale blue petals.

At the end of the aisle, Caitlin is collected by Justine's parents. Braden gets to go stand with his father. I'm the third bridesmaid to walk out, just before Justine. As I slowly make my way down the aisle, my eyes are drawn to Will. My step falters as I get a good look at him. Will looked incredible in his charcoal suit the night before, but now, in his tux, he looks devastating. When his eyes lock onto to mine, I feel my breath catch. The tuxes for the groomsmen are classically styled. His is well fit across his broad shoulders and narrows towards his waist to show off his build. Even though I'm far away, I know the blue iris at his lapel matches his eyes. I wonder if I have a similar effect on him when I see him chew on the corner of his bottom lip. I make it to the front of the church and slip into my place in line. I watch as Justine makes her way down the aisle and laughs when Braden leaves his dad to go stand next to her.

When Christine and her father approach us, I look at Brian and feel a tug in my heart as I watch his face break into a beautiful smile just for her. The service is not long, with one reading of Love is patient and a blessing from the pastor before Brian and Christine say their vows. When it is time to kiss the bride, Brian dips her dramatically while we all cheer. I'm so happy until it hits me how much I wish I was on Will's arm instead of the groomsman next to him. Justine holds Braden's hand and links her other arm through Will's before they follow the bride and groom. Curtis, Justine's husband, and I walk out together. Once we're outside of the church, Will approaches me, holding out his arm. In a daze, I link mine through it, and he rests his other hand on my elbow. My vision blurs when he starts to run his fingers back and forth across my skin.

"You look beautiful, Sarah," he whispers.

"Thank you. You look," I gulp. Hot, sexy, droolworthy, "nice too."

I realize what I'm doing and try to pull my arm away, but he doesn't let go. I tug at it again and shoot him a look. He shakes his head and ignores me. I'm saved by Cindy, who collects me for some bridesmaid group photos. We go back inside the church and take multiple group shots. I do my best to avoid Will until we are paired up during a full bridal party group shot. It is hard to concentrate, and I hate myself for how my heart starts pounding when he stands behind me with his hands on my waist. When the photographer asks us to move outside, I feel Will's fingers grip me tighter. I look back at him and glare. He loosens his grip and follows me to the steps of the church, where we take more group photos. Afterward, I look around for my parents. They're my ride to the reception.

I look up at Will. "I'm supposed to ride with my parents."

"I already talked to them. You're riding with me."

"What?"

He shrugs. "I need to talk, and you need to listen. Pretty sure you won't jump out of a moving car."

"My clutch?"

He smiles, turns us around, and walks me to the room we were in before the wedding. I don't see the point, but he still holds onto my arm. I grab my clutch, and he leads me out to his car, opening and shutting my door for me. I buckle my belt and fold my hands in my lap as he walks around the car. He slowly backs out and pulls onto the road before he says anything.

"Sarah, what did Jessica have to do with you leaving?"

"I thought you were going to talk, and I was supposed to listen," I huff, looking out my window.

"Please answer me."

"What, you're so surprised I found out?" I hiss.

"Alright, let me just say this one time. I have no idea what you are talking about."

I spin my ring. "So are you trying to say Jessica didn't go with you to Italy?"

"She did, but—"

He pulls into the country club, which is thankfully on the same street as the church.

"Don't, just don't." I breathe, looking out my window.

The second he's parked, I'm out the door and speed racing toward the entrance. He's right behind me, so I dash into the ladies' room, hopeful he won't follow me. I call Sawyer.

"Aren't you supposed be at the wedding?" she asks.

"Wedding is over. I am now hiding from Will in a bathroom at the reception."

"Sarah!"

"I hope you know I am not proud of myself."

"Alright. Time to put on your big girl panties and go talk to that boy. Seriously, Sarah, you are hiding in a bathroom."

She's right. I know she is. I still wait another fifteen minutes before peeking out the door to see if he's there. He isn't, so I make my way into the ballroom.

Chapter 16

Past

"You are so beautiful," Will whispers in my ear as he slips my corsage onto my wrist.

I love the dress Brian helped me pick out. It has a beaded halter-style neckline and falls elegantly to my ankles. I see Will's eyes widen when he notices the hidden slit up the side. My hands shake as I pin his boutonniere to his lapel. My mom takes a million pictures of us before she lets us leave, then takes even more pictures of us getting into Will's car. Will pulls me into his lap once the door is shut behind us. I freak out, thinking my parents can see us, until he reminds me of the tinted windows. Prom is being held in the ballroom of the community center. By the time we get there, Will has kissed off all of my lipstick, and I have to reapply. After we walk in, we have our pictures taken again under an arch made out of balloons. A bunch of kids from our class are going to an after party at Bravo's house. We are not.

Will got us a room at a hotel. He picked one out of the way so it would feel more private. We're both ready to leave but are only staying for the prom court announcement. Will doesn't care, but I think he's going to be named prom king, and I don't want him to regret missing that. I wait off to the side when the prom court is called up onto the stage. I meet Will's eyes and grin when he blows me a kiss. My smile falls a bit when I notice Jessica glaring at me. I'm grateful when they dim the lights to announce prom queen, until they call her name. I'm not surprised. She's gorgeous, her blonde hair tumbling over her bare shoulders and the top of her strapless red gown.

When they call Will's name for prom king, I can't help but smile at his goofy expression. He looks around the room until his eyes rest on me. He laughs when I give him a wolf whistle. I'm less thrilled when I remember the prom king and queen dance together. I have to look away when Jessica wraps her arms around his neck. When I turn, I see Kyle, her date, watching them dance. He looks just as uncomfortable as I feel. I glance back at Will and Jessica, my mouth dropping. I watch Will jerk his head to the side as she tries to run her fingers through his hair. I look back at Kyle to see him shake his head and walk away. I jump when I feel an arm around my waist and look back to see Will.

"What are you doing?" I whisper, feeling everyone watching us.

He pulls me out onto the dance floor where Jessica still stands, her mouth open. "I'd rather dance with you."

I can't argue with that, but as much as I dislike Jessica, I do feel bad for her as she hurries off the dance floor in search of Kyle. The dance floor fills around us as Will brushes his lips across mine. The crown is a bit big and has a decidedly lopsided perch on his head. It matches his lopsided grin. We leave after that dance. Will laughs when I make him walk out first. I feel like if we walk out together, everyone will assume we're going to go have sex. We are. I just don't want anyone to know. He is pulled around front, waiting for me. He's leaned up against the side of his car. I'm suddenly shy as I walk over to him.

He cups my face and kisses me. "We don't have to do anything. I'd be happy to just fall asleep with you in my arms."

"I know."

He opens my door for me, and once I'm seated, closes it and jogs around to the driver's side.

"I mean it. We can just kiss and stuff if you want."

"Will, I'm nervous but I want to, so let's go."

He doesn't argue with me and drives to the hotel. We're both eighteen so getting the room isn't an issue. Will came earlier to book it and already has the keycard. I wonder if people are watching us as we walk across the lobby to the elevators. Will has a duffle bag slung over one shoulder and my hand in his. I put my other hand on top of them, and Will looks down at me.

"Are you sure about this?"

I blush and bump my hip into his. "Stop asking. I'm sure."

He bends down to kiss me, his lips not leaving mine until we reach our floor. When he opens the door, I cover my mouth with my hands. There are rose petals covering the bed. Will pulls a lighter out of his pocket and walks around the room lighting candles before plugging his iPod into a speaker.

"I made a playlist I thought you might like," he says, pressing play.

The first song that comes on is “You're Beautiful.” He stands over on the other side of the bed, pulling off his suit jacket. I'm still standing by the door but start to move towards him. He meets me halfway and runs his hands up and down my arms.

"Do you like it?"

"I love it. Thank you."

"I want it to be perfect for you."

"As long as I'm with you, it will be."

He pulls me closer, kissing my forehead. "I love you so much."

"I know. I love you too, so, so much."

I turn in his arms and pull my hair to one side. "Can you unzip me?"

His breath catches, and his hands tremble as he slowly lowers the zipper of my dress. I shiver when he drags his fingertips up my arms, pausing to kiss my shoulder. He takes a step back as I lift the halter strap over my head. I turn back to face him, holding my dress to my chest. When his eyes snap to mine, I let my dress fall to the floor. I didn't wear a bra because of the neckline of my dress, so I lift my arms to cover my chest. He closes the space between us, pulling me into his arms. I reach up to untie his bow tie and giggle when I see it's a snap on. He moves his hands from my back to help me unbutton his dress shirt. He's pulling it down his arms and tugging his undershirt off as my hands move to the button of his slacks. We're both undressed and on the bed before the next song comes on.

We lay there, facing each other. We've never been all the way naked, both of us, either of us, together before. This is the first time I'm actually seeing him. Will catches my eye and smirks. He knows I'm checking him out.

"Can I touch you?"

"Huh?" He hesitates. "Sure."

He turns onto his back and puts his hands behind his head. He watches me nervously. I reach out to touch him, a nervous stroke up the length of him. Snapping my eyes to his, "Is that okay?"

His jaw is tense. He's chewing on the corner of his mouth. He doesn't say anything, just nods. I reach out again, this time to grasp him. He groans, his hips twitching. I release him and pull my hand back, apologizing.

"It's okay. That felt really good."

I giggle. "God, I thought I hurt you."

I gently explore him with my fingertips until Will admits he might lose it if I keep touching him. He pulls me up to kiss me, turning back onto his side, pressing against me.

"I'm nervous I won't be good at it," I say, avoiding his eyes, spinning my ring.

He cups my face in his hands, lifting it until my eyes meet his. "Impossible."

"Will it be messy?"

He laughs, dropping his hands, and then tries to keep a straight face. "Why would it be messy?"

I cover my face. "Because I've never done it."

He's so quiet I move my hands to look at him. He's grinning at me.

"What?" I laugh.

"You're cute."

He licks his lips before crushing his mouth to mine. We blur into a mesh of arms and legs. I feel full of him and also surrounded by him. It's like inside and out there isn't a spot of me that isn't marked by him. I'm mesmerized by his face, a face I thought I knew every expression of. I learn a new one today as I watch him fall apart. Afterward, Will still above me, I laugh out loud when I realize I'm no longer a virgin.

Will stills. "Something funny?"

"You just deflowered me." I try to keep a straight face and fail.

He just grins down at me and replies. "Did it hurt?"

"A little at first, but then it felt better." I run my hands up and down his back. "Was I okay? For you?"

"Okay? Sarah, you crazy beautiful girl. I love you so much. That was the second best moment of my life. The first was when you told me you loved me."

"So that's a good thing, right?" I tease.

He shakes his head at me so I kiss him, pulling him down so that all of his weight is on me. He's sweaty. I'm sure I am too, but I love the way he feels, the way he smells. I don't know why, but I start giggling. He lifts his head to look at me.

I cover my mouth with my hand. "We just did it, Will."

He laughs. "Why is that funny?"

I can't stop. I'm shaking. "I just can't believe it."

"I love you, even when you're a crazy person." He brushes his nose against mine.

"I've loved you for so long," I confess, laughter gone.

He reaches up to smooth some hair from my face. "How long?"

"Seventh grade."

"You did not." His eyes widen.

"Alright, maybe it wasn't love love, but I had the biggest crush on you."

"I never knew. I never thought—" He just shakes his head, then lowers it to kiss my neck right below my ear before saying, "I wish I had known."

"Why?"

"We could have gotten together sooner."

Chapter 17
Present

I go find my seat and hesitate when I see Will's arm resting on the back of my chair.

As though he senses me, he looks back at me. "Fall in?" When I ignore him, he goes on. "So I went over with Brian this morning to help pick up your wedding gift. Pretty big coincidence out of everything they registered for, we picked the same thing."

He pulls my chair out for me, and I sit. Seeing a server, I order a drink. This is going to be a long night. I'm on my second drink by the time food is served. I have only taken one bite before the DJ announces the arrival of the new Mr. and Mrs. Miller. We all stand and applaud as they walk in hand and hand. They come and sit down to eat while Justine and Curtis go to the center of the ballroom to give their toasts. It's cool to hear more about how Christine and Justine met.

They met in elementary school, the first day of fourth grade. During roll call, they say that they were the only girls in the class whose names ended in 'ine'. Once they learned how close they lived to one another, they formed a club and called themselves the Ine's and would not let anyone else join unless their name also ended in it. Justine had everyone laughing as she cringed and said they were only fourth graders and that was as creative as they got. Curtis lived next door to Christine growing up and hated them. He moved towards the mic to confirm that, yes, he did in fact hate them. Brian had only known Curtis as long as he had known Christine, but it was Curtis and Justine's approval that clinched the second date for Brian in the beginning. Curtis tells a very funny story during his toast of when he pulled Brian aside to explain the whole 'Ine' thing to him and make sure he knew Justine was not a best friend. She was a sister to Christine. It had been clear to both Justine and Curtis how much Brian cared for Christine, and they gave him their blessing before he even knew he was going to propose.

After they finish their toasts, other people clink their glasses and make toasts. Christine's father makes an especially sweet one that brings tears to many eyes. He speaks of how Christine is not only his only child but still his little girl and he can rest because he knows Brian will spend the rest of his days doing everything in his power to make her happy. Since my father is not much of a talker, his toast is perfect for him. He raises his glass. "To the bride and groom. Your mother and I love you both very much. Welcome to the family, Christine."

I tense when Will stands and gives his toast. "I work with Christine and have known Brian forever. He saw me having lunch with Christine one day and had to meet her. In our infinite wisdom, we came up with a plan to get them together. It was clear there was something there when Brian called me after their first date and could not stop talking about her. He told me he thought she was the one. I remember telling him to tell her that, to make sure she knew every day just how much he loved her and how she was the only one for him. Don't make the mistake I did and let the one get away. He took my advice and almost scared her away by coming on too strong. Moral of the story, given my romantic history, is they were clearly meant for each other, considering I got involved and they're still together."

When Will sits back down I look at him, almost not surprised to find his eyes on me. This whole week has been so strange. I have never felt closer to that night than I do now. I never stopped loving Will. I just tried to throw myself into my work to ignore it for all these years. I just feel so confused by Will. It's clear he still feels something, but what? Is the whole reason he made such a big deal about wanting to talk to me so he could have a chance to apologize? Well, I don't want his apology. You don't get to break someone's heart and think everything is fine just because you say sorry. That's just not fair.

I turn my head back to the dance floor when the DJ announces the first dance. Christine's dress has loops and buttons to secure the train to the back of her gown so she won't have to worry about anyone stepping on it while she dances. I'm trying so hard to be happy for my brother, but it's hard. When you're busy, it's easy to ignore couples and romance. The only days that really suck for me are Valentine's Day and June 17th, the anniversary of that night. I signal the server for another drink. With any luck, I'll be numb before the night is over. Will catches my eye when the server hands me my drink and raises a brow. I give him a half smile and take a drink. I start to second-guess my plan to get drunk when I start imagining Will's lips on mine. I push my drink away and pour myself some water. I need to stay in control tonight.

Brian comes to ask me to dance after the father daughter and mother son dance. I'm happy for an excuse to get away from Will. Brian is so happy. I can't help but relax during our dance, until I see Will move behind him and tap Brian on the shoulder.

"May I cut in?"

I shake my head, but Brian has already given Will my hands. The look they exchange as Brian walks off the dance floor makes me wonder if they planned this. When Will's hand slides around my waist and he pulls me to his chest, I forget what I was thinking about. Will was always a great dancer. He leads me around the floor smoothly as he looks down at me. I want to look away, I do, but instead I drown in the sea of his blue eyes.

He seems just as captivated yet cautious, like he knows I'm thinking of running away again. A big part of me wants to but Sawyer is right. I need to grow up. I'm not that young girl who ran away in the first place. I've changed, and maybe it's time to finally free myself of this pain that I have held onto for so long.

When the song ends, we stand together as the next song starts before I start to pull away. I've regained my ability to think again and am fighting an internal battle with myself on whether to throw myself at Will or put as much distance between us as humanly possible. I'm scared of how I still feel for him.

Part of what scares me so much is I don't know what he wants from me. Since I've been here, he's only said that he wants to talk, and he's asked me why I left. In the toast he just gave, when he said he let the one get away, did he mean me or Jessica? She's engaged now. He could have been talking about her. Will takes my hand, and we walk off the dance floor together. Instead of taking us to our seats, he walks us out into the lobby. He doesn't let go of my hand.

"Sarah, what did you mean when you said Jessica was the reason you left?"

"I leave the day after tomorrow, Will. What's the point in even doing this?"

"What's the point? Sarah, you broke my heart when you left, and you tell Brian I don't get to hurt. I think I deserve to know what happened."

I snort. "I broke your heart?" I sink into a chair behind us, talking about this is going to be harder than I thought. Will pulls another chair around and sits so he's facing me. He puts his hands on my knees, and I put my hands on his. Here goes nothing.

Chapter 18

Past

Since prom, we have become even more inseparable, if that's even possible. As excited as I am to graduate today, I am also dreading Will's trip to Italy. I twirl in front of the mirror one last time before going downstairs. I'm graduating today, and Will and I are going to Bravo's party tonight at his parents' lake house. Will is driving me over to the school, and my overnight bag is packed. I have my gown on, but it isn't zipped, and I'm carrying my cap. Will is being lectured by my mother about being responsible tonight.

"Forgetting anything?" Will asks.

I mentally go over everything I've packed before hurrying back upstairs for my phone. Will catches my eye at the bottom of the stairs and winks at me when my mother isn't looking. I'm wearing a new dress, and it's shorter than anything else I've ever worn. I blush when I see him check out my legs. He takes my bag, and I go give my mom a hug. My parents and brother are meeting us over at the school and taking Will and I out to dinner before we leave for the party. My mom walks me out to Will's car, which annoys me because that means I'll have to wait to really kiss him. He pulls his camera out from the backseat and takes a picture of my profile as I wave to her. When we back away, he puts his hand on my thigh, making me tingle all over. He's grinning because he knows the effect he has on me. I elbow him when he turns off of my street. He pulls over onto a side street and kisses me. My hands are in his hair, and part of me wants to climb into his lap. When he breaks our kiss, his eyes are glazed, and he's breathing heavy. I'd laugh, but I probably look the same way.

"Do we really need to go to this?" he jokes.

I wrinkle my nose at him, and he turns the car around. When we get to school, we kiss again before we are separated alphabetically. I'm between Jordan Mason and Russell Morgan. We shuffle along in line until all our parents and family have been seated in the gym before our class walks in. The applause is intense. I look around, wondering where my parents are sitting. I remember where we sat when Brian graduated, but I don't see them there. I look around for Will and grin when I find him, and he blows me a kiss. Our principal and teachers are on a stage at the front of the gym. He welcomes all of us and gives a speech about hoping we all rise to the potential that is within us.

He turns the mic over to our class valedictorian, who turns out to be a girl I have never seen. I look back to Will and raise a brow. He laughs, shaking his head. I guess he doesn't know who she is either. Her speech is short and sweet. I still have no idea who she is, but I'm a fan of her not taking forever. I cannot say the same for the keynote speaker. I miss his name, but he apparently graduated from our school and is now a writer somewhere. I fiddle in my seat. My ass is asleep, and if I do not stand up some, I may have to hobble across the stage.

I think the whole auditorium breathes a sigh of relief when he finishes. Row by row, our class makes its way across the stage. Our row stands when the last person from the row ahead of us heads towards the stage. Standing gives me enough time to feel blood circulate again, so I'm not walking like an idiot. I'm nervous enough that I'm wearing heels. My biggest fear is tripping onto or off of the stage. My step almost falters when I hear Will shout my name. I grin in his direction and hear a wolf whistle. I wonder if he did it. Somehow, I manage to accept my diploma and move my tassel without doing anything silly. I'm back in my seat when Will crosses the stage. He's popular, so the applause he gets is huge. I scream as loud as I can and hope he hears me. The only funny part of accepting our diplomas is when JJ goes up to get his. He pauses to kiss every female teacher on the cheek.

Once our whole class has their diplomas, our principal declares us graduated, and we all yell and throw our caps in the air. I have my name written in mine, and somebody hands it to me a couple minutes later. Our parents empty the stands and come to take pictures. As a mass, we start to make our way outside where there is more room. I see Will across the way with his parents. I start to walk over, but his mom gives me a weird look so I find my family instead. We take a ton of pictures and then even more once Will walks over to join us. He hugs me and gives me a sweet kiss in front of my parents. This dinner is going to be torture.

I walk over with Will to his car. We're meeting my parents at The Cheesecake Factory. When I take off my gown, his eyes widen, and he shakes his head. He's wearing a navy blue suit with a light blue shirt and patterned tie under his gown. When we're both in the car, I look to make sure my parents aren't around before I grab him by the tie and kiss him. I can't wait to go to Bravo's. Will keeps his hand on my thigh as we drive to the restaurant, his thumb moving slowly back and forth. His touch does something to me. I wonder if he feels the same way.

We have a short wait for our table. Will sits next to me, and I gasp when he puts his hand on my thigh again, grateful for tablecloths.

"Are you alright, dear?" my mother asks.

"Oh, um, my seat is cold." I shiver.

"It is cold in here," my father agrees. "You should have brought a sweater."

Will slips off his jacket and helps me put it on before putting his hand back.

"What a gentleman," my mother gushes at Brian. Will moves his hand further up my leg.

He chokes on his water when I return the favor and put my hand in his lap. "Are you alright?" my dad asks.

Will gulps then says, "Fine, sir. Just went down the wrong pipe."

"So polite," my mother gushes over Will. "Don't you think Sarah looks pretty tonight?"

"Mother," I shriek.

Will squeezes my leg. "Yes, Mrs. Miller. I think she looks beautiful tonight and every night. I'm the luckiest guy in the world."

My mother looks at me with an expression like, 'see, even Will says you're pretty.' I roll my eyes. If she only knew. Will's hand stays on my leg our entire dinner. We are so stuffed my parents end up taking our cheesecake to go so we can eat it tomorrow. Outside of the restaurant, we all hug before Will and I take off. I notice Brian saying something to him so I ask him about it once we're in his car.

Will cringes. "He told me he's going to chop off my hand if I can't keep my hands to myself and that he's not ready to be an uncle."

Will laughs at my horrified expression and puts his hand back on my leg. It's a thirty-minute drive out to the lake house. I am Will's navigator and read off directions from a print out Bravo gave him. It makes me happy to know he's never been here. I've always heard these parties can get a bit crazy. I press the button to open the sunroof and tilt my chair back to look up at the sky for a couple minutes until I need to pay attention to road signs again. The driveway is already overflowing when we get there. Will parks a ways down the street. I reach into my bag and pull out some flats to change into. He carries both of our bags in one hand and takes my hand in his other. Bravo's name is really Brett, but his dad is military and is teaching him the letters for his name like Bravo, Romeo, Echo, Tango, Tango. Brett liked Bravo so much his dad started calling him that, and soon so did everyone else. I had never been to one of Bravo's parties. They are always invite only, and while Will is always invited, he never goes.

Will finds Bravo and finds out what room we'll be staying in. Bravo gives Will a key to lock it, telling him to keep it locked so other party goers don't try and use the bed. Eww. When Bravo leaves, Will locks the door behind him and tackles me.

"You look so hot," he groans in my ear as he kisses my neck.

I tug on his hair until he pulls back to look at me. "Kiss me," I demand, wrapping my arms around his neck as he lowers his lips to mine. He's on top of me, but he still doesn't feel close enough. I loosen his tie and start unbuttoning his shirt. Once it's unbuttoned, I pull it and his undershirt loose from his pants.

He stops me. "Sarah, why don't you go to Gainesville or Athens Tech, and we can get a place together in the fall?"

I wiggle out of his grasp and stare at him openmouthed. "Did you just ask me to live with you?"

He tugs me back towards him and holds me close. "I don't know how to be away from you."

"I just—" I don't know what to say. I know I love him, and I know he loves me. Will Price just asked me to live with him. What's funny is, dating or not, my parents would probably be all for it. But he's supposed to be living in the dorms this year. "I can't live in your dorm. Besides, the whole point of me staying home is to save money."

"I'll pay for everything."

"Alright, Daddy Warbucks. We both know that is not happening."

"Do you not want to live with me?" He starts chewing the side of his lip.

"Of course I do."

"Then we'll figure everything else out." He he starts tucking his shirt back in. "We should probably go downstairs for a little while."

"Let's just stay here," I plead.

"Nope. You are going to that party. I just need to give you a giant hickey first."

I swat at him and pull away, shaking my head. He gives me his best pout until I lean forward and nibble his lower lip. He looks shocked for a moment, then kisses me fiercely. I just want to stay here.

"Let's make a deal," he suggests, rolling me over onto my back.

"What kind of deal?" I whisper as he lies on top of me.

"We go to the party for an hour and then hurry back here for the rest of the night."

I press my hips against his. "Why don't we just not go out there and stay in here all night?"

He chews the corner of his mouth before dropping it to mine. "You drive a hard bargain."

I'm just about to ask him if that means we can stay in when the doorknob to the room turns.

I gasp, but Will says. "Don't worry. It should be locked."

Then we hear a knock and Bravo on the other side. "Are you guys coming down or what?"

I roll my eyes when Will calls out. "We'll be down in a few." He looks back at me.

"Well, I guess it would be rude to stay up here the whole time," I admit. "One hour?"

"One hour," he confirms.

It feels like everyone's eyes are on us as we walk down the stairs to the party. Will has my hand in his, and I cling to it. He has to sense I'm freaking out because at the bottom of the stairs he drops my hand and puts his arm around my shoulder, pulling me flush against him. We can hear Bravo's booming voice in the kitchen and head that way.

When he sees us in the doorway, he smiles. "Wasn't sure if you guys were ever coming out of that bedroom. Damn."

I turn my face into Will's chest as I feel my cheeks redden. Will lifts my chin with his fingers and drops a sweet kiss on my lips. His expression so vulnerable, I put my arms around his neck and pull his lips down to mine once more. Will gets a beer and grabs me a cola. We walk around for a bit, his arms never leaving my shoulders.

In each room we walk into, Will makes a point to talk to everyone and ask about their plans for the summer. I shake my head, trying not to laugh at him, but I love it. He's only doing it so they'll ask what his summer plans are, and when they do, he pulls me closer and tells them he plans on spending every spare second with me.

Vanessa, a girl from my calculus class, chimes in. "Are you guys going to stay together once you leave for school?"

Will doesn't hesitate. "Yes, and don't worry about us. We'll make it. Plus, I'm trying to talk her into coming with me."

After he has made sure every person at the party is crystal clear that we are together, we make our way out onto the back deck. It has a wooden walkway built off of it that leads to a dock. We walk out on to it and sit together on a bench. There is a clump of trees off to the right of the deck, and Will points out the occasional firefly. There is a full moon out, and we watch its reflection dance across the surface of the lake. It is beautiful with the exception of some bugs, intent on making a meal out of me.

"Has it been an hour yet?" I joke.

He rolls his eyes, and we head back towards the house. I don't know why I feel so out of place. I know almost everyone at this party. It's just that I know I wouldn't be here if it wasn't for Will. He had always offered to take me parties when we were still just friends, but it never appealed to me. Before kissing him was an option, I'd rather just hang out with him at my house or go get ice cream. Will is talking to a couple of guys he had played lacrosse with. I excuse myself to find a bathroom. He asks if I want him to come with me, which makes me laugh because I'm pretty sure I can handle it.

I find Bravo and ask him where the bathroom is. Once he tells me, I'm glad I asked. I never would have found it on my own. The bathroom had been a later addition to the house and built in underneath the staircase. I'm washing my hands when someone knocks on the door. I hurry to dry them and open the door to turn the bathroom over to whoever knocked.

"Well, if it isn't SPT."

I don't say anything, and Jessica rolls her eyes. "So where's Will?"

I shrug and turn to walk away. The last thing I want to do is get into it with her tonight.

"Did Will tell you?"

I look back. "Tell me what?"

Just then, I feel an arm wrap around my waist and look up to see Will glaring at Jessica. She smiles and goes into the bathroom.

I nudge him with my shoulder. "What was that about?"

He shakes his head. "Ignore her."

I laugh. "I try. She just makes it hard to."

Will's arm is back around my shoulder, and we walk into the living room. A couple girls from our class come up to say hi to Will. One of them, Jordyn, seems to be almost flirting with him right in front of me.

She rests her hand on the forearm of the arm not around me. "Will, I can't believe you and Jessica broke up." She glances at me.

He lifts his arm and rubs the back of his neck so she isn't touching him anymore. "We did. You know Sarah and I are together now, right?"

She plasters on a fake smile. "I always thought you guys were just friends."

"Definitely more than friends."

"Aren't you going away to school, Will?"

"I am." He pulls me closer to him.

She nods. "I just always heard that long distance relationships never work."

He feels me stiffen against him and looks down at me. Keeping his eyes on mine, he says, "We'll be fine."

Bravo comes up behind Jordyn and rests his chin on her shoulder. "Dude, Will, you need another drink. Sarah, you drinking?"

I shake my head and walk with Will so he can grab another beer. There are a couple of guys doing keg stands. I've never done one, not that I have any plan to, especially in a dress, but it's fun to watch. When one guy drops down, I turn my head to say something to Will, but before I do, his lips are on mine. I turn in his arms, coiling mine around his neck as he straightens, lifting me. Even though we are in a crowded room, all of that noise and distraction just falls away. His lips, his tongue, his hands gripping me all overwhelm me. My eyes open and look into his as he slowly lowers me till my feet are back on the ground.

He presses his forehead to mine, eyes locked, as people whoop around us. Bravo pushes a cup into Will's hand. His eyes flick up to him, and he nods and thanks him before placing a soft kiss on my lips. I lean my head against his chest as he drinks his beer. He's standing tall with his shoulders back, his free arm around my back. He feels warm and smells really good.

I look up at him. "Has it been an hour yet?"

He grins, pulling me towards the stairs.

"Aw, come on, guys," Bravo calls out behind us. "You guys aren't going upstairs already. The night is young."

We ignore him, only focused on each other. Will locks the door behind him as I lay across the bed, laughing when he takes a running start and leaps onto me. Since our first night together, our times together have been rushed, stolen moments while our parents aren't home. We take our time tonight, exploring each other since there is no reason to rush. Will knows my every expression, how to make me fall apart and put me back together again. I know him too, his body, his scent, the look that crosses his face, and the way he holds his breath right before he explodes. We eventually fall asleep coiled around each other.

Sometime during the night, we both start at a loud knock on our door.

Will reaches over to flip the light on. "What the—"

"Will, man, open up." We hear Bravo through the door.

Will pulls on his boxers and gets out of bed, and I pull the covers closer to me. He cracks the door. "What's up, man?"

"Dude, I'm so sorry to bother you, but someone fucking hit your car."

"Fuck," Will hisses. "Give me a minute to get dressed. I'll be right down."

He closes the door in Bravo's face. I get out of bed and start to get dressed.

"You don't have to come down, babe," Will says as he pulls his pants on.

"I know. I'm coming anyways."

I grab my purse in case I need to call Brian for help or anything. Once we're both dressed, we leave the room, Will locking the door behind us. I hold his hand as we make our way back downstairs. The party is still going strong, and we get a few knowing looks as we pass people, making it clear everyone knows what we were doing. We go outside and walk over to where Will's car is parked. Even in the dim light from the houses we can tell his car is not in the same position it was when he parked it. There is another car parked crookedly on the other side of the street. The back passenger side, behind the door, is dented.

"I am so sorry, Will." Claire Warner approaches us as we get closer to his car.

I can see now the other car is hers and has a similar dent, only on the driver side. Looks like she backed right into him. Will tells her it's fine, and they exchange insurance information. Will unlocks his car for me to sit in when I start getting eaten alive by bugs again. I'm sitting in the front passenger seat, messing with my phone when Jessica opens the driver's side and gets in.

"What are you doing?" I jump, dropping my phone between the console and the seat.

"Just felt like chatting. So Will popped your cherry, didn't he?"

I put my hand on the handle, ready to just get out.

"He told you about Italy, right?"

I pause, looking back at her. "What about Italy?"

"I'm going with him. He didn't tell you?"

"You're making it up."

She pulls out her cell phone, holding it up so I can see a text message from Will.

So happy you are coming to Italy with me. We never should have broken up. I'm breaking up with SM before we leave.

I stop breathing. My head feels really heavy, and for a moment, I think I'm going to faint.

"I don't believe you. You faked that somehow."

She passes me her phone. "You don't think that's from Will? Why don't you press call?"

It's still on the text. There's no way. I hit the menu button and press call. I hold the phone to my ear. I turn. I can see Will through the window. Two rings. I see his phone isn't ringing. I knew she was—wait, he's reaching into his pocket. He looks at the caller ID. He fucking smiles.

"Hello?"

I hang up the phone and drop it on the console. I'm frozen until I see her phone light up. Incoming call. Will. I look up at her, and she's smiling at me. God, I feel so stupid. I grab my purse and jump out of the car. I hear Will call my name, but I'm running towards Bravo's house. I see a couple kids I know getting into a car.

"Are you guys going home?"

"Sarah Miller?" Christie asks.

"Yes, are you going home?"

"Ah, yeah. Are you okay?"

"I have to get out of here. Can I get a ride?"

Chapter 19

Present

I look up at him. "Remember how the bugs kept biting me so I sat in your car while you were exchanging insurance info with Claire?"

He nods, chewing on the side of his bottom lip.

I take a deep breath, lifting my hand to spin my ring. "Jessica got in the driver's side and told me about Italy, showed me a text you sent her."

Will shakes his head. "She lied. I didn't even know she was going until we got to the airport."

I glare at him. "She showed me a text from your number that said how happy you were she was going. That you made a mistake breaking up with her."

I go to push his hands from my knees, but he grips them tighter. "Sarah, I never sent her a text, and I sure as shit did not regret breaking up with her. I didn't know her family was going to Italy until I saw them at the gate. I swear."

"Her family? She never said her family was going, and I saw the text and then she had me call the number from the text, and you answered and when I hung up you called back."

"Yes, her mom, dad, and little brother. I have no clue what to tell you about the text. I know I didn't send it, and I don't remember a call that night, but I was freaking out about what my parents were going to do when they saw my car. If someone, anyone called, I probably answered, and if they hung up, I probably called them back."

We sit in silence, looking at each other. He seems so upset. I start to wonder if maybe Jessica somehow faked the text. Also, she had said nothing about her family going. That doesn't seem as bad as just her going by herself with Will's family. Maybe if I had known that I never would have left the lake house that night.

"Was there anything else?"

I close my eyes, trying to block out the memory of what really made me run.

"Please, tell me what happened."

"I need a drink, maybe two."

"If I go get you drinks, will you still be here when I get back?"

I nod. I have lived with this for too long. I'm finally going to get it off my chest. He's back with my drinks, or rather shots, in no time, and I see he has a couple for himself. He hands me one, and we lock eyes before throwing them back. Rum. I put my hand out for the second shot once the first is down.

"Where did you go that night?" he asks, taking the glass and setting it with the others on a table behind his chair.

"Christie Howell and some other girl were leaving. I had my purse and got a ride home with them."

Will looks angry. "I was losing my mind when I couldn't find you. I thought maybe someone had taken you, or you had fallen into the lake or, I don't know." I pale as he drops his head into his hands.

"I didn't think. I just had to get out of there."

"Why didn't you say something to me. I would have proved to you it wasn't true, whatever she said."

"I just never could believe you would want someone like me more than someone like her," I admit, looking down.

After a few moments, when he hasn't said anything, I look up at him. His head is in his hands. I reach out to touch his hand, and his hand grips mine. He lifts his head and meets my eyes, his expression tortured.

"Will?" I ask.

"I thought you knew how much I loved you." He shakes his head. "How could you not know?"

I go to tug my hand from his, but his grip only tightens. "I didn't. I couldn't. You were the most popular guy in school. Every girl loved you. I still don't—"

"Stop." he holds up his hand. "Don't even go there. I didn't care about all of the stupid high school shit, and you knew that. You knew me. When I couldn't find you, I've never been more scared in my whole life. I must have called your phone a hundred times before I figured out it was in my car. I finally called Brian, and he told me you came home crying. I almost drove over right then, but he told me to let you sleep and that we could talk in the morning. Bravo took my keys and wouldn't let me drive anywhere until the next morning because I was so freaked out. And then when I got to your house you were gone."

I never knew where my phone had ended up that night. I had my purse on me and had left everything else behind. I had held back tears the drive back and pretended to be asleep when Christie or her friend talked to me. Once I was home, I cried myself to sleep. I knew Brian heard me come in and that he heard me crying. I remember him standing on the other side of my bedroom door, asking me to let him in. He finally gave up and left me alone, and I cried myself to sleep.

The ballroom door opens, filling the hallway with music. I look up to see my uncle Chip walking out of the ballroom and over to us "You kids okay?"

I nod. Will just keeps looking down.

He looks at Will. "Are you sure?"

"We're just talking." I look back at Will. "It's okay."

Chip heads back into the ballroom, the hall filling once again with music until the door shuts.

I had turned my head to watched Chip leave. When I look back at Will, his eyes are on me, their expression weary.

"Seven years, Sarah. Did we really lose seven years because of a text?"

I hesitate and then shake my head.

"Then why?"

My insecurity over Will's feelings for me are the reason I left the lake house that night after Jessica talked to me, but that wasn't the whole reason I left.

The hall fills with music again when someone walks into the hall, in search of a restroom most likely. I look at Will. "Can we talk outside?"

He nods and stands, still holding my hand. We make our way to the front entrance, then follow a stone path along the left side of the building to a covered patio. There are ceiling fans slowly creating a slight breeze and black wrought iron tables and chairs. It's June. In Atlanta, the shade is welcome, but it's still humid. Will releases my hand and shrugs off his jacket, resting it over the back of a chair before pulling another chair out for me to sit in.

I'm nervous. I'm not sure I can actually tell him what happened. "I need to walk around if that's okay. You can sit. I just can't right this second."

He lowers himself into his chair.

I pace back and forth, nervously in front of him, jumping when he shouts, "Sarah, just tell me."

I quickly nod, thinking back to that morning.

Chapter 20

Past

I wake up feeling like shit. My head is pounding from all of the crying I had done the night before. Plus, I cannot stop thinking about Jessica and that text. Part of me doesn't want to believe, can't believe it. Will had told me he loved me. I want to trust him. I want there to be some way to explain what was on her phone. I go to the bathroom to wash my face. Looking in the mirror is not helpful in that moment. I am a red splotchy mess. What guy would ever want to be with me when they could be with Jessica Burton?

That and the fact that she'll not only be going to Italy but college with him in the fall is killing me. I should probably end things with him. That would be the safest thing to do. Break up with him before he breaks up with me. God, what if the entire thing had been some sick joke. Where he makes me think he loves me, and then he gets back together with Jessica. I have no idea if any of this has actually happened. It just seems to be the most likely worst case scenario that keeps playing through my mind.

There is a part of me that rebels against the idea, that remembers Will asked me to go away to school with him. Maybe he does care for me, even love me, and all I'm doing is overreacting to something he has no part of. Can't I trust him? He had been my best friend for so long. I don't really think he would ever do anything to hurt me.

I spend the next half hour trying to figure out where my phone is so I can call him. It isn't in my purse, and I start to suspect I may have lost it somewhere at the party. One downfall of cell phones is not knowing anyone's number by heart. I cannot remember Will's number and finally find a student directory. It doesn't have his cell phone number in it, but it does have his parents' home number. I can at least leave a message with his mom or dad, hopefully his dad, for Will to call me once he gets home. I owe it to him, after everything that we have been through, to talk to him about what Jessica said. I'm really hopeful that his dad will answer. Ever since she caught us by the pool, I've been weirded out by his mom.

I dial his number and cringe when his mother answers. "Price residence."

Shit! "Um, hello, Mrs. Price. Is Will home?"

"His name is William. Who is this?"

Like they don't have caller ID, I think to myself. "It's Sarah Miller."

"Why didn't you call his cell phone, Sarah?"

This is not going well. "I can't find my phone and can't remember his number. If you could give it to me or maybe just let him know I called?"

"I'm sorry. I can't do that, Sarah."

Um, what? "Pardon?"

"I'm not going to give you William's number or tell him you called."

"Why not?"

"I know what you are after, Sarah, and I'm going to tell you right now you are not good enough for my son."

"But—"

"There is nothing you can offer him. He is going away to school, and it is time for this relationship of yours to end."

"But I love him."

"Sarah, I am sure you are a nice girl, but William deserves better. Someone who has been brought up the same way as him."

"He doesn't care about any of that." I'm frantic.

"Maybe. But he does care a great deal of what his mother and father think. Which is why we have invited Jessica Burton to come with us to Italy."

"Why?" I just don't understand.

"Sarah, let me make this clear. You are not the type of girl William needs in his life. If you continue this, whatever it is, with William, we won't pay for his college. Is that what you want?"

"Please...no."

The line is dead. She hung up on me. I stare at the phone in my hand. What just happened? Could they really refuse to pay for his school? That would kill him. And that stuff about Jessica. It's true. She's going with them to Italy. I set the house phone down on the kitchen table and slump into a chair. This is not happening. This cannot be happening. All I want to do is crawl back into my bed and never come out of it again, but I also feel this overwhelming need to get as far away from Decatur as I can. I cannot see Will. At worst, he's dumping me for Jessica, and at best, we can't be together anyway because his parents won't pay for his school.

Something across the room catches my eye. It's a picture on the refrigerator of my uncle Chip sitting on his motorcycle. I just figured out a place to go to. I quietly make my way upstairs to my room and pack everything I can into my backpack, and an old duffle bag. I really hope Brian will forgive me someday for what I'm about to do. I load my stuff into his piece of shit Ford Escort and grab the envelope from a birthday card my uncle sent me. I hope he meant it when he said I'm always welcome. I write my parents a note and leave it on my bed so they won't worry, with a P.S. at the end to Brian to apologize for stealing his car.

I leave Brian's car parked at the train station. I lock the keys in it, but my mom has a spare set so he should be fine. I'm pretty sure my uncle lives near Trenton, so I buy my ticket and wait for my train. The wait isn't long, which is good because I have been staring at the front entrance for the past hour, expecting my parents to walk in. The one thing going for me is that they probably don't even know I came home last night and won't be missing me for another couple of hours. By that time, I will be well on my way to New Jersey. The train is half full, but more passengers board than depart every stop we make. I purposely pick a seat near the bathroom so I won't have to worry too much about my duffle.

The seat next to me is empty, thankfully. An older woman across the aisle tries to small talk with me, but I pretend to sleep so she'll leave me alone. I'm feeling strangely like none of this is real, like I haven't just run away from home. Like last night never happened, and I'm going to wake up at home in my own bed and things with Will will be the same. Somewhere in Virginia, I get up and visit the dining cart, unable to avoid my grumbling stomach any longer. I get a sandwich, some chips, and a juice. Back at my seat, I struggle to get it all down. I was so hungry before, but now that I have food right in front of me, I can't seem to eat it. Everything makes me think of Will. If he was here, he would be hogging all my chips and trying to steal my pickle.

The only reason I manage to finish my lunch is because concentrating on eating is somehow keeping me from crying. The train is fuller now, and I know in the next stop or so I may lose the empty seat beside me. I relax after the stop in D.C. when enough passengers get off that I think I might make it the whole way without having to sit next to someone. Instead, in Baltimore, I meet Sawyer, which seems like a strange name for a girl, but it suits her. She's my age, or maybe a year older by my guess, and also heading to Trenton. I haven't told her that's where I'm going because I haven't been able to get a word in edgewise other than my name.

I feel like I'm grayscale sitting next to her. She seems almost Technicolor with her cotton candy toned streaks peeking out underneath her white blonde hair to her facial piercings and half sleeve tattoo on her left shoulder. It's cool on the train, and I wonder if she's cold in her black tank top with the giant Rolling Stones mouth on it and cut-off jean shorts. There is so much going on with her I'm not sure where to look. She's compact too, maybe three inches shorter than me and skinny. I bet she could skip a meal if she was heartbroken. She talks with her entire body, tapping her foot, wildly gesturing with her hands, tilting her head from side to side.

I start to wonder if she's high or naturally hyper. She seems to have no fear talking to me, or anyone sitting near us. She's moving to Trenton to live with an ex-boyfriend because she caught her current boyfriend, well now ex, getting head from their neighbor. The ex she's going to live with only offered her a place so he would have a chance to get in her pants again. She shrugs when she says that, almost saying she wouldn't mind that either. As she talks about what a royal ass her current ex is, I stare at her tattoo. It's on the shoulder farther away from me, and I can only see half of it. She catches my eye and turns so I can get a better look at it. It's an elaborate blue-feathered bird, its wings on fire.

"It's a phoenix," she says, looking down at it, her right hand raised to trace its outline with her fingertip.

"Beautiful," I say. "Did it hurt?" I've always thought about getting one.

"It hurt in some places." She points to a section on the underside of her arm. "Mainly it felt like rough rubbing, if that makes any sense. Not like getting a shot at the doctor. You scared of needles?"

"I wouldn't say I'm scared of them, but I don't like them," I admit.

We continue like this until we have to get off and switch trains in Philadelphia. I crack up when she seems surprised I get on the same train as her. I still haven't told Sawyer I'm going to Trenton too. When I show her my ticket, she beams and insists that we hang out once we both get settled.

I must have fallen asleep at some point because Sawyer shakes me awake when reach Trenton. It's three o'clock in the morning, and she offers to let me crash on her ex's couch so I can try and figure out where my uncle lives in the morning.

She just has to clear it with her ex, Jake. He is waiting in the station for her, and she runs to him and jumps into his arms. He's tall and muscular, with shaggy brown hair that reminds me of Will. He's awake enough to pick her up and spin her around. I predict make up sex in their future. When Jake sets her down, Sawyer pulls him over to me and clears the whole couch crashing plan. He nods to me in greeting and asks Sawyer where she's sleeping if I'm on the couch.

"I'm sure I can find someplace," she says, winking at him.

He grins and pulls her suitcase with one hand and carries my duffle in his other. He drives a beat up, single bed truck. After tossing our bags in the back, we climb in, Sawyer sitting in the middle.

During the drive over Jake looks over at me. "Are you in trouble or something?"

"Huh?" I'm tired, so I'm not sure what he's asking.

"Why doesn't your uncle know you're coming?"

I sigh. "I haven't told anyone."

"So," Jake continues, "are you in trouble?"

"Like with the law? No. With my parent's for taking off probably and my brother. I kinda took his car without asking, but I left it at the train station so—"

"How old are you?" Sawyer squints at me.

"I'm eighteen, so relax. I just had to get away."

"Why?" Sawyer rubs my arm.

I look at the side window, blinking away tears. "Um, that's a long story."

"We got time, Yoda." She gestures at my Star Wars t-shirt.

The story doesn't take as long as I thought it would. By the time we are at Jake's apartment, I've told them all about Will, Jessica, and what his mom said. I start crying about halfway through and am now hiccupping as I get out of the truck. Sawyer walks beside me, rubbing my back as Jake grabs our bags from his truck.

Jake drops my duffle and backpack next to an ancient looking sofa in his living room. Sawyer digs through her bags in search of tea to make me a cup. She says it will help. My throat feels like I gargled sandpaper after talking while crying so tea sounds nice. I settle down on the sofa and wait while she microwaves water. Jake is standing in the doorway of his bedroom, probably wishing Sawyer was not occupied with me. The sofa is soft but kinda smells like feet, so I pull out a hoodie from my bag to sleep in. I'll wait until Jake and Sawyer go to bed to put it on. I don't want to offend Jake, but I also don't want my hair to smell like feet when I wake up.

Sawyer brings me my tea, and I tell her and Jake I'm fine and to go ahead to go to bed. Jake must not be scared I'll steal any of his stuff because he does just that. Sawyer lingers a moment or two longer before following him. I pull out my iPod to drown out the sounds of their getting reacquainted. I fall asleep listening to an audiobook of the first Harry Potter book. It's narrated by an English man, and I love his accent. I'm three quarters in when a patch of light from Jake's sliding door to his balcony wakes me up. I quietly freshen up as best I can in Jake's bathroom. It feels good to change into clean clothes even if I didn't take a shower.

Since I don't have a phone to call a cab, I decide to wait for Sawyer to get up to see if I can use hers. Jake comes out of the room first, in just his boxer shorts. He must have forgotten I stayed the night because his eyes widen, and he darts back into his room when he sees me sitting on his sofa. Sawyer comes out next, grinning and stretching. She's wearing a strapless sundress, Jake follows her shortly, in jeans and a t-shirt this time. When I ask if I can borrow a phone to call a cab, Jake asks to see my uncle's address.

"This isn't far." he glances at Sawyer. She raises her eyebrows at him. "We can give you a lift."

I relax into the sofa. "That'd be great. Thank you."

"Did you want to call your folks? Maybe get your uncle's number and make sure he's home first?"

I groan, instantly tense again. Time to face the music.

Chapter 21

Present

"She wouldn't. She—"

I turn and glare at Will. "You believe whatever you want, Will. You asked why I left, and I told you."

I turn to head back inside, but he grabs my arm, stopping me. He's behind me. I turn slowly to face him. His lips are on mine before I know what's happened. It's like no time has passed. My body is still his. Will's arms grip my waist while I wrap my arms around his neck. He tastes like rum and cinnamon. I want to consume him. When he breaks our kiss, we each take a step back to catch our breath.

"You can't just kiss me," I pant.

He ignores me. "You didn't leave because you didn't love me?"

I shake my head. How could he ever think I didn't love him? Will sinks into one of the chairs and puts his head in his hands, his breath ragged. I sit in the chair next to him, unsure of what to do. I gasp when I see tears in his eyes and move to wipe them away.

"I've loved you and only you, Sarah, for the last seven years. When you left, you broke my heart."

"I didn't know. I thought I was doing the right thing. That you didn't love me as much as I loved you."

He took both of my hands in his. "Don't ever say that. Don't ever think that."

My eyes water when his voice breaks. All this time. I feel like a fool. He pulls me into his lap and crushes me to his chest. His lips find mine again, and I'm lost. Nothing will ever keep me from him again. We melt into each other, and the world slips away for a little while until we both turn our heads towards the sound of someone clearing their throat.

"Anything you two want to tell me?" Brian asks as he leans up against a post.

Will grins at him over my shoulder. "I'm in love with your little sister."

"Really?" I ask.

He kisses the spot below my ear. "Always."

"About fucking time." Brian laughs before heading back inside.

"But you don't even know me anymore, and I don't know you. We can't just jump into something like this. I live in Denver. Seriously, what are we going to do?" I ask, trying to be logical.

He's now nibbling my ear lobe. "I disagree, Sarah. I know you. I know your favorite sandwich. I know your favorite book. I know what you look like when you are sad and you don't want anyone to know. I know how much you loved your Grandma Bess, and I bet you still have her picture by your bed. I know where you're ticklish and that you love waffle cones. I know you hold your breath when you think your heart is racing and that you've done that every time I've been near you this week. Don't think that we're rushing or doing anything too fast, and about the other stuff, we'll figure it out. I want you to know that I will do anything to be with you."

I pull back, putting my hands on his chest, hesitating when I can't help but wonder what he looks like without a shirt on, before shaking my head. "Will, you make it sound so easy, but I still have to leave. Do you want a long distance relationship?"

He chews the side of his lip. "Don't go."

I laugh. "Oh, it's that easy. What about my job?"

He shrugs. "I'm sure they'll get by without you for a while."

My mouth drops. "Will, it's my company."

His eyebrows come together. "Like you own it?"

I smile and nod. Guess he didn't know everything about my life in Denver.

"You own a company?"

I shrug. "It's not a big company, but yes, it's mine, and this is the longest I've ever been away. I really do have to go back."

He lifts my hands and positions them back around his neck. "I could come back with you. It's summer break."

My eyes widen. "You would do that? Really?"

He leans forward to kiss me. "I'm not letting you get away from me again."

I'm thrilled. I am but, "What about your mom?"

He takes a deep breath before his eyes meet mine. "I've done all I can for her. I'm not even sure she'd notice if I left."

"Don't say that," I object, not that I know any better. I just can't imagine that.

"It's true. I hate to say it, but she hasn't been right since Bethany's death. I don't know why she said what she did to you, but I believe you. I'm so sorry she did that, that Jessica did that. Please know that you have always been all I've ever wanted."

When his lips move to my neck, I ask, "Should we head back inside?"

"Nope, don't want to."

I laugh. "William."

He looks up when I say it and smirks, releasing my waist. I daintily step off of his lap and smooth my skirt. He stands, hooks his jacket over one shoulder with one hand, and takes my hand in the other.

As we walk off the patio, he looks down at me. "Just think if you would have talked to me the first day you got back."

I elbow him. When he grunts, I smile sweetly up at him. I hate how right he is. I had been so positive that my feelings for him were one-sided. I hadn't even given him a chance. I'm somewhat amazed he kept trying to talk to me, considering how I acted.

Once we're back in the ballroom, he drops his jacket off at our table and pulls me out to the edge of the dance floor. "I think you owe me a dance, Miller Lite."

As we make our way onto the dance floor, Lucky by Jason Mraz and Colbie Caillat comes on. I stop and put my hand over my thumping heart. This song used to kill me whenever I heard it. Today, I have never felt luckier to be in love with my best friend. I don't notice that the dance floor has cleared while we dance until the song ends, and I hear everyone clapping. Will kisses my forehead as Brian and Christine come over to hug us.

"Finally got her to talk to you." Christine laughs as Brian puts his arm around her waist.

I blush. "Guys, this is your day. Please don't make a big deal about this."

"Me make a big deal?" Brian hams as he walks over to the DJ and borrows his mic. "Hey, everyone. Let's give a hand to one of my best friends, Will, and my baby sister, Sarah. Will has only been in love with her forever, and it only took like a decade for him to seal the deal. To Sarah and Will."

"To Sarah and Will," everyone exclaims raising their glasses.

I turn my head into Will's chest. He lifts my chin and sweetly kisses me as everyone around us cheers. The rest of the evening, we are almost as popular as Brian and Christine. First, my mom and dad come over to gush about how they always knew we would end up together, and now this means I'll be moving back home. Will is trying not to laugh at me as I bite my lips and sweetly nod at every crazy thing that comes out of my mother's mouth. When she brings up children, my father pulls her away after I shoot him a pointed look.

Once they're out of earshot, I raise my drink and say, "Well that wasn't awkward, was it?"

Will just laughs and kisses me. How is he so calm about all of this? We dance, and kiss, and can't seem to stop touching each other. His hand is either on my shoulder, or thigh, or holding my hand. When Brian and Christine leave, we join everyone outside in throwing birdseed as they get into the limo. They're staying in a local hotel overnight and leaving for their honeymoon in the morning.

Will turns to me once the limo pulls away. "Want to get out of here? We can get a room."

Oh my god. "Um, I," I stammer.

I want him. I do. I'm just not sure I'm mentally ready to do anything with him just yet. He sees my hesitation and pulls me into a hug.

It's like he can read my mind. "We don't have to do anything."

He says that, but I have a feeling that is exactly what will happen if we're alone together in a room with a bed. I'm not sure if it's a good idea, but I don't want to leave him either.

"What if we lay down some ground rules?" I suggest.

He chews on the side of his lip. "What kind of rules?"

"No sex."

His eyes widen, and he glances up at the sky, taking in a breath before looking back at me. "Not sure I can agree to that one."

I close my eyes. Something about the way he says that makes me picture him on top of me. Think of something else, sep-iras, Keogh plans, employer sponsored contributions. I open my eyes and lick my lips. The look in his eyes as he watches my mouth is not helping. I cannot be thinking of having sex with Will right now. This entire day has been crazy. I just need to clear my head.

"Will, I just don't think we should rush."

His hands cup my face. "As you wish."

I smile at his Princess Bride reference, but inside, I hope he really means it. As much as I want to throw caution to the wind and drag him to the nearest hotel, I am scared. I worry that Will isn't grasping how difficult this may be. I've been on vacation this week. Normally, I work at least seventy hours a week, and I love it. I have done this to myself. I used work to replace Will, and now that he's back in my life, I'm afraid I won't be able to balance everything. Will had always been the spontaneous one. Me? I'm a planner. He threw out the idea of him coming to Denver like it's no big deal, but how will he feel if I'm gone sixty percent of the time for work?

"Could we go somewhere and talk?"

He smirks at me like talking is the last thing he wants to do right now but shrugs, and taking my hand, pulls me over to my parents.

"Mr. and Mrs. Miller, I'm kidnapping your daughter."

My father isn't paying attention, but my mother beams and gives us a very saucy look. Mom! I shake my head and put my hand up when Will starts to say something. I'm processing the fact that my mother seems thrilled I'm leaving Brian's wedding with him. Will just seems smug. We go back inside to grab his jacket and my clutch. As we drive to my house, Will rests his hand on my thigh. The sensation of his hand there feels so familiar but new at the same time. On the drive back to my house, Will texts Brian to see if it's cool if we hang out at their place. Will has a spare key, and they're staying in a hotel for the night. Brian seems to talk for a long time, but Will doesn't tell me what he says, just that it's alright for us to go over there.

Will follows me up the stairs and watches me as I throw some things in my carryon bag for the night. It's like he doesn't want to let me out of his sight, so I'm not surprised when he trails me into the bathroom. I grab my toiletries and pause to meet his eyes in the mirror. I cannot believe this is happening, that we are happening. The last time I was as scared and excited at the same time was when I was with him all of those years ago.

I want him, but even admitting that to myself is frightening. I start to pull the pins from my hair. He sits on the edge of the tub as I work at removing them before getting up to help me. His hands in my hair feel heavenly, and I'm pleasantly surprised to see there is less hairspray in my hair than I expected.

"Sarah." My brown eyes meet his in the mirror. "Has there been anyone since me, you know, for you."

"In what way?" I'm not sure what he's getting at.

He's chewing on his bottom lip. "sexually."

I pause, my hands dropping. "Have I had sex since you?"

He drops his eyes and nods.

There is no point lying. "Yes, I've had relationships over the last seven years, Will." I hesitate. "Have you?"

He looks up and nods.

"So," I start. "Neither of us has anything to be worried about, right? Just," I take a deep breath. "Did you get back together with Jessica after I left?"

He makes a face. "No way."

He grabs one of my hands and kisses it. When the last of the pins is out, I close my eyes and lean back into Will's chest as he drags his fingertips over my scalp and through my hair before resting them on my shoulders. My eyes flutter open as I watch him in the mirror, his expression hooded as he slowly sweeps my hair to one side and lowers his lips to the back of my neck. I melt against him and reconsider my no sex ground rule before pulling away.

"You stay here or go downstairs. I'm going to change out of my dress."

He starts to follow me. "You sure you don't need help with that."

I try to keep a straight face and point down the stairs. He pouts but turns and slowly makes his way down them. I go back to my room and pull on some jeans and a v-neck t-shirt, purposely avoiding anything with easy access. The less of my skin Will has the opportunity to touch, the better. Tonight is going to be all about talking about what happens next. Talking, not action. I pull out my phone and call Sawyer.

"Just so you know, I've been fucking dying for an update."

I laugh. "Well, I have a big ass update." I pause, just to piss her off.

It works. "Sarah, I swear to God. Spit it out already."

"So, I talked to Will, and I think we're dating now."

"Shut the fuck up!"

I shake my head. "No lie. He's waiting for me downstairs right now. He's been in love with me this whole time and says he'll come to Denver for the rest of the summer."

"Aww. That makes me want to cry. Wait, the whole summer? Is homeboy unemployed?"

I snort. "No, he's a teacher. You know, summers off."

"I'm going to get to meet him. Just so you know, I'm happy dancing."

I didn't expect anything less. "But I have to go. I will tell you more later. I love you."

I hear her making kissy noises as I end the call.

"Who do you love?"

I look up to see Will leaned up against the doorway. Mental picture. God, he looks hot in his tux. I'm almost regretting not wearing something more revealing.

"Spy much?"

He shrugs.

I walk over to him and slip my arms around his waist. He rests his chin on my head. "It was Sawyer, my new best friend."

I feel him tense and look up at him. "What's wrong?"

He's chewing on the side of his mouth. "What's he like?"

I get a dirty look when I laugh at him. "Will, Sawyer is a girl. All better now?"

He avoids my eyes.

I smack his chest. "You were jealous." I laugh. I have no idea why I find this so funny.

He silences me with a kiss that makes my knees feel weak. He raises his lips from mine. "Yes, I was jealous. I just happen to know your last best friend fell in love with you, so I got nervous."

I meet his gaze as he dusts another, more delicate kiss across my lips.

Chapter 22

Past

The telephone call to my parents sucks. My mother asks why I was trying to scare her to death and demands I come back home immediately while my father tells me he's disappointed in me. I hold firm, though. Then she says Will had come over looking for me and that I need to call him.

That's when I start to cry. "We broke up, mom."

"What happened?"

"I don't want to talk about it. I just need to get away. Please, can I have Uncle Chip's number?"

Hearing the desperation in my voice must do it. She gives me his number. I call him next. He's surprised but said he meant it when he said I could always stay with him. Just hearing that makes me exhale. I had no idea what I was going to do if he had said no. Jake and Sawyer drive me over to his house a short while later. I write down their numbers, and my uncle gives them his land line number. Sawyer makes me promise we will hang out.

The first weeks are awful. I can't help but stop and wonder what Will is doing. In Trenton, I'm not just mourning a broken heart. I miss my best friend. I had lost my cell phone that night so Chip eventually offers to add a line on his plan. My new number now starts with 609 instead of 404. I close my Facebook account, not that I used it that much before. I just can't risk seeing him. To a certain extent, I disappear. That's the start of my new life. My uncle lets me use his other car to get around. I get a job at a local coffee shop and go to school. I have a couple of weird conversations with Brian when he brings up Will, but after I make it clear I have nothing to say on the subject, he stops bringing him up.

I get registered at the local community college. While I wait for classes to start, I spend a lot of time with Sawyer. She's adamant that I should call Will and hash it out but also respects the fact that I'm not going to. Besides, he's in Italy right now, with Jessica. Just thinking about that kills me. I try to stay busy, even trick myself into thinking I'm moving on a couple of times. It was all a lie, I tell myself to make it through each day without him, but deep down, I know you never really get over your first love.

I had never been the best student, but something drives me to put everything I have into my classes. Every time I think about slacking off, I hear Mrs. Price's voice in my head telling me I will never be good enough for Will. That thought seems to push me more than anything else. After some time, I'm certain Will is probably back with Jessica or maybe even with some other girl at the University of Georgia. I know there is no future for us, but I never want to feel not good enough for someone ever again. I even go on a couple a dates with a guy who works at the coffee shop with me. His name is Carl. He's nice, but I don't feel anything when he kisses me.

It's just before the start of my second semester, and I am working the afternoon shift at the coffee shop when a regular comes in. Her name is Helen, and everyday at three she stops in for a coffee to get her through the rest of her day, or at least that's what she always says. She's an accountant and works in the same building as the coffee shop, just three floors up. She's extra frazzled today and keeps staring at me while she sits, drinking her coffee. The fact that she is sitting at all is odd. She normally just takes her order and leaves. We're slow, so I grab a spray bottle and walk around the counter to wipe down the tables.

When I get closer to her, I ask. "Everything okay?"

One side of her mouth pulls up, and she clears her throat. "Funny you should ask. My assistant quit this morning. She's moving to Mexico to find herself."

Helen is a total corporate Barbie, from her rust shaded pantsuit to her low blonde power ponytail. She puts her elbows up on the table and steeples her fingers before resting her chin on them. "Any interest in becoming my new assistant?"

I shoot her a questioning look. "What?"

She picks up her coffee and takes another sip. "I'm serious. I know you're in school, and I can work around your schedule. I have seen you in here almost every day and can see how competent you are. Plus I'll give you health insurance."

It isn't the health insurance that I'm interested in but her appearance of success. I want that. I end up taking a fifteen minute break and talk to her more about what exactly she's looking for. I tell her I'll think about it and that I want to talk to my uncle about it. She finishes her coffee and leaves. Since it's Friday, I have until Monday afternoon to think about it. I watch her walk out of the shop, a guy holding the door for her as she leaves and watching her as she walks away. She not only has that air of success but of confidence too. If I had to guess, I would say she's in her early thirties, but she seems younger.

I think about her job offer for the rest of my shift. It's probably a no brainer but I've become comfortable with my current routine. I know what's expected. I know I can handle my course load and my shifts at the coffee house. This opportunity has a whole lot of unknown to it for me. Chip's not home when I get off of work. It's Friday night, and he's likely with his latest arm candy. Our conversation will have to wait until tomorrow. When I first moved in with Chip, I wondered if my living with him was affecting his social life. I learned pretty quickly I wasn't and have gotten very good at making conversation with his conquests every Saturday morning.

Chip's making some eggs, and Allison, his latest lady, is sitting at the breakfast bar in his robe when I walk in. She was here last weekend too. He must really like her. I mumble a greeting to the both of them before pouring myself some orange juice and sitting on the stool next to Allison. I tell them all about Helen and her offer. Chip and Allison are both realtors. They don't work for the same company but had met at an open house for one of Allison's clients. They work with accountants regularly and are familiar and impressed with the group Helen is in.

Chip says it's the kind of place I would be lucky to get my foot in the door. That in itself is an overwhelming concept. I'm still in my first year of school. Do I even want to put my foot in any doors yet? That whole 'what do you want to be when you grow up' question still plagues me. I do not know the answer. I'm not even sure when I will know the answer, but I do know I want to be a success. Now, knowing more about the group Helen works for, I decide to go for it. It's the decision that changes my life.

Helen's thrilled when I give her the news on Monday. My current boss, Danny, is less excited but still wishes me the best. My first few weeks with Pickering, Coleman, and Van Arsdale are awful. Moving into the world of finance is not unlike learning a new language, one that includes a lot of numbers. As promised, Helen does work around my course schedule. This job consumes me in a way that at the end of each day I'm so mentally exhausted, I collapse into bed. I'm almost too busy to think about Will. Almost.

He's every brown-haired boy to me. Sometimes I question my sanity, so certain I see him in a crowd. I still check his horoscope every day, crying myself sick whenever it mentions romance. I wonder what he's doing, and if he ever thinks of me. I want to be angry at him. I will myself to be. Thinking of him in that way feels safer for me. I embrace my role as the injured party. Is that fair? Probably not. It's self preservation. That and avoiding any conversations that involve my going home. I use my schedule as a crutch, as my reason I just cannot go home. It's only partly true. I am busy but I accrue vacation time so I have the option available to me. Instead, I bank my vacation time to take time off during finals.

The real reason I don't want to go home is Will. I have submersed myself in Trenton, almost using this city as a blanket. The distance protects me both from knowing what anyone is doing back home to having anyone know about me. I want to be forgotten. I want to forget them. My parents come out to visit me a couple of times while I'm in school. I get my fear of flying from my father. They would probably come out more often if it had not been for that. Brian comes out to visit me once. It's the year after I graduate and start sharing an apartment with Sawyer. She's out of town visiting some friends in Canada.

I'm still working for Helen but now full-time. Brian's in his grunt years at his law firm and is enjoying the break. It's summertime, and we go hiking. I remember him complaining about his retirement plan at work. His company is going away from the pension-style plan to a heavier 401k-style with discretionary additional contributions from his employer. He's annoyed because the paperwork is a mess. Then something had been misfiled, so he would be missing the additional deposit this year.

That's not the first time I had heard that type of complaint. Working with Helen, who specializes in dealing with complex tax filings, I know how important a qualified contribution can be to someone's tax liabilities. There are so many different types of retirement plans out there that many of her clients don't know until after meeting with her that another type of plan may have been more favorable for them. Many of Helen's clients never follow up on the recommendation of establishing a different type of plan because all of the paperwork seems too daunting. That's when I have the idea of creating a service to do that part. I learn after talking to Helen that my idea is not unique. There are companies, or individuals, in existence who already do this. Doesn't mean they can't use a little competition.

Chapter 23

Present

He's quiet on the ride over to Brian and Christine's condo. He laughs when I press the button to open the sunroof. I shrug and cross my arms across my chest. I'm trying to have an open mind, but I'm more scared than I care to admit. What if this doesn't work out? Not tonight, but in general. I never truly got over Will. I cannot imagine trying to again. I sit there, actually thinking how feasible it can be to run my company remotely from Georgia or move it out here altogether. I stop thinking when I notice Will is parking. I look up and hesitate. I'm nervous about being alone with him.

He can tell I'm about to say something. He leans over to kiss me. "Shut," he punctuates each word with a kiss, "up."

I bite his lower lip, and he stills. I release his lip and meet his gaze.

"I've been dreaming about having you in my arms again for seven years, Sarah."

I don't trust my voice and am blinking wetness away from my eyes. I mouth 'me too.' He gets out and walks around to open my door. I feel a bit awkward walking into my brother's complex without him.

"Did you know I used to live here?" he asks, taking my hand in his.

"Christine told me. She pointed out your old place form their balcony. Said something about you and Brian trying to play catch between both places."

He laughs and rubs his hand over his face before smiling down at me. "It was fun living here. I miss that place."

His thumb sweeps back and forth across the back of my hand as we wait for the elevator.

He leans and kisses the spot right below my ear. "'Member that thing I said about you holding your breath when you think your heart is pounding?" My eyes flick to his. "You're doing it right now," he whispers in my ear, then laughs when my mouth drops open.

We both look up at the sound of the elevator's arrival. Will captures my mouth the moment the elevator door closes behind us and doesn't release it until it dings to let us know we've reached our floor.

I push off his chest. "Remember we're just talking tonight."

He nods, but his eyes say another thing altogether. He takes one of my hands from his chest and pulls my bag behind us as we walk to the door of Brian and Christine's place. Their place seems smaller with Will inside it, his height making the high ceilings seem less so. Maybe it's my feelings towards him.

"Want a drink, Miller Lite?"

I have to laugh. "No one has called me that in..."

His hands cup my face. "Seven years?"

I nod as he lowers his lips to mine. I lose myself for a moment before turning my face away from him.

"Will, we need to talk."

His lips move to my jaw line. "This is more fun."

"Will, I leave the day after tomorrow."

He nips my earlobe before pulling back and smirking at me. "Drink?"

I need a clear head. "Just water."

I sit in one of their armchairs while Will goes to the kitchen to get our drinks. He makes a face at me when he sees where I'm sitting. I sat here on purpose so he can't touch me. His fingers brush mine as he hands me my glass. He sets his beer on the coffee table and removes his bow tie. I watch riveted as he tugs his dress shirt from his pants and unbuttons it. He has a white undershirt on, and once his dress shirt is off and draped over the back of the other armchair, he sits on the sofa and takes a drink of his beer.

Neither of us had said anything while he was taking it off, and I feel uncomfortable now having stared at him so intently while he did it. I flush, turning to look away, and take a loud gulp of my water.

"Alright, Sarah. Let's talk."

I take a deep breath and let out a whoosh of air. "I'm scared, Will." There, I said it. "This whole thing scares me. I have no idea what we're doing, and it's all happening so fast, and then there's the fact that I live in Colorado and you live here and you have your hands full with your mom. You have to know I'm a planner. This not knowing what is going to happen is not something I'm good at."

He quietly chews on the corner of his mouth and stands, walking over to me and scooping me up into his arms before I can react. He turns and walks back to the sofa as I wiggle and complain in his arms.

He sits, holding me in his lap, his lips at my ear. "I'm scared too, Sarah, but I know that this is going to work out. You and I are going to happen. There isn't anyone else for me. I'm not going to let you run again, I'm not. Things might suck for a bit while we figure all the details out, but we can't let that stop us from being together. Did you ever think we would have a normal relationship? Does that even exist? Our feelings are as real as it gets. When I kiss you, it's real. I know you feel it too. I feel like I've been sleep walking for the last seven years, and then I saw you on the plane, and it was like I was awake again."

I sag against him. I want to believe him. I do.

He eases back further onto the sofa, and I move with him, my head on his chest.

Trailing his fingertips up and down my back, he goes on. "I was wondering if you'd tell me more about your company. How many people work for you? Is there any possibility of you moving here and working remotely?"

I nervously spin my ring as I think about it, Will patiently waiting for me to say something. "Counting me, there are five of us. I guess it doesn't really matter where I'm based because of all the traveling I do. I'm usually out of the office at least three days a week anyways. I just don't know. My team is more than just employees to me. They're my friends. I think I need to wait until I'm back home to talk it out with my team. We've talked in the past about not renewing the lease on our office space and working remotely instead. Maybe I could move back if I did that." I look up at him and see his grin. "Don't get too excited. I'm just throwing out ideas. I want to talk with my team first."

He doesn't stop smiling and leans forward to kiss my forehead. "It'd mean a lot to me if you would come over tomorrow and talk to my mom with me."

I tense, and he feels it. "Please, Sarah."

"I'm not sure that's a good idea, Will."

He rubs his hand through his hair and sighs. I hate that I'm still intimidated by her, even after all of these years. Her words still cause me pain, but I have to think about Will and what is important to him.

"If you want me to, I'll go," I say after some time.

He crushes me to his chest. "If I want you to? Does that hold for everything?" His voice is husky in my ear.

I laugh. "You are impossible."

His lips move to my neck. "Haven't we talked enough?" he murmurs against my skin.

"Will." He ignores me. "Will!" Still ignores me. "WILL!"

He lifts his head. "Yes, dear?"

"We're not going to do stuff on my brother's couch."

I gasp as he stands up, taking me with him. "It's cool. They have a spare bedroom."

He carries me across their foyer and pushes a door open with his foot. The room is dark. He shuffles me as he raises his elbow to the wall switch. There's a queen-sized bed flanked by a bookcase and a desk. Will gently lowers me to the edge of the bed, kneeling in front of me. His hands are on either side of my face as he kisses me. When he nibbles on my lower lip, I giggle, and Will pulls back to look at me.

I shrug ."Sorry, you're just always biting your lip. Now mine too?"

The corner of his mouth pulls up. "Kind of kills my trying to seduce you when you laugh at me."

"Oh, that's what's happening here?" I tease.

I yelp as his hands grip my waist, pulling me off the bed and onto the floor with him. I'm now on my back, Will's lips fused to mine. Gone are the gentle kisses from only a moment ago. His mouth feels almost primal in its claiming of mine. My knees are bent, Will's hard body between them. His weight alone on me is making me writhe against him like a horny teenager. He takes my hands and holds them in one hand right above my head. His other hand is making its way up the inside of my shirt. I gasp when he palms me over my bra, and he raises his face to look at me. I'm panting and arch my back, encouraging him to go on. He licks his lips as he looks down at me, knowing what he's doing to me.

I jerk my hands from his grasp and tug at his shirt. He sits back on his heels and pulls it forward, over his head. I scramble up, slack jawed to look closer at the tattoo on his left pec. My fingers trace over the old school Miller Lite logo as he looks down at me.

"When?" I ask, raising my eyes to his.

"Bout seven years ago."

His breath catches when I lean down to kiss it. He groans and fists his hand in my hair, dragging my lips back to his as he lowers us back down to the ground. I push against his chest to stop him halfway. He pulls back confused, his eyes widening as I pull my shirt off and lay down. He shifts down to kiss my stomach, my hands tangled in his hair. I buck when he nibbles my side, and he chuckles against my skin. I pull on his hair, and he moves upward to worship the skin exposed above the cups of my bra, his hips grinding against mine. I arch my back and pop open the clasp, his fingertips dragging the straps down my arms. His lips never leave my skin. My hands move to his shoulders, my nails digging into him as his tongue circles me.

His hand cups me. His thumb strokes me as his lips move to the base of my neck.

"Will, kiss me," I beg, missing his lips.

His lips crash into mine, his tongue invading me with fervor. He lifts me and leans my back against the end of the bed, my legs straddling him. I feel his arousal, and I push against it. He groans against my mouth, his hands in my hair. He lowers his lips again, blazing a trail down my neck to my chest. He drops one hand to cup and tease one side while his mouth tortures the other, switching between them as my head falls back onto the bed to give him more access. I freeze when one of his hands drops to the button on my jeans.

"Is this okay?" he murmurs against my skin.

I mumble yes. I think. Maybe not because he asks me again. I lower my hand to unbutton it, pushing his hand away. His hands grip my waist as he lifts me up onto the edge of the bed. I fall on my back as he picks up my feet, one at a time, and slips off my flats.

"You're gonna wanna hold on," he says as he lowers the fly of my jeans. I cover my face as I feel them slide down my legs. Once they are off, his hands come back up to rest on the waistband of my underwear. He hesitates until I lift my hips. He pulls them off quietly and drops them. I feel exposed and press my legs together. He tucks his hands behind my knees and tugs me closer to the edge of the bed, gently opening my legs. In vain I reach for a pillow to cover my face with as I blush.

"You have no idea how long I've wanted to do this again," Will murmurs, his lips hot against my thighs.

I gasp, arching my back. His hands come up to grip my hips, as he begins to consume me. I'm wound so tightly it shocks us both at how quickly I break, my body trembling. Will is suddenly over me, wiping tears I didn't know I was shedding from my eyes. I want to tell him I'm fine, but I can't seem to form the words. He folds me into his arms and strokes my hair as I sob into his chest. This day has emotionally kicked my ass. Exhaustion sweeps over me, and I drift to sleep hearing Will whisper he loves me.

Chapter 24

Past

On my first trip to Colorado, Sawyer tags along. She's been to Denver before and wants to introduce me to some people. One person in particular, Jared. Sawyer is certain that he will be the one to make me forget all about Will. Plus she has a thing for his roommate, Caleb, so that helps. I'm still a one person enterprise and on a budget. Having a free place to crash while I attempt to woo prospective clients is the only reason I can afford to make the trip. I have meetings scheduled the first two days but can relax the rest of the week.

Jared picks us up from the airport, and Sawyer's eyes light up when she sees I think he's cute. My tell, I'm so busy looking at him I half walk into a pillar in the parking deck. It barely catches my shoulder and I think I play it off well, but she's on to me. She pushes me towards the front passenger door of Jared's Tahoe before jumping in the back and acting all innocent. As we're driving to their apartment, I start feeling really hot, and I'm worried that maybe the windy roads are giving me motion sickness. My ass feels like it's on fire. I shuffle in my seat and discretely try and fan myself.

Jared looks over at me. "Are you okay?"

His concern makes Sawyer pop her head between our seats to look at me. "Sarah?"

I flush. This is embarrassing. I don't want to have to admit I'm feeling queasy. "I'm just warm," I mumble noncommittally.

"Do you want me to turn off the seat warmer?" Jared asks, his hand poised over the button.

"Oh my God, I thought I was losing my mind. Yes, please turn off the butt heater."

Sawyer collapses into convolutions in the backseat while Jared tries to keep a straight face. I roll my eyes. It's not like either of their asses were on fire. In fact, I'm feeling a little miffed that I received no heads up that my butt was going to be artificially baked. I shuffle in my seat again as my rear returns to room temperature. Jared looks over at me again. Why do I always have to act like a spaz in front of cute boys? Once his eyes are back on the road, I have a better chance to discretely check him out. He's tall. I can't really tell if he's muscular or not since he has a snow jacket on. He seems fit, though. He's wearing a knit hat, so I'll have to wait until we're back at their place to see what his hair looks like. He has pale brown, maybe hazel, eyes and an adorable crooked smile.

I can totally see why Sawyer thinks I'd like him. I can't deny I find him attractive. Hopefully, I can make it through the next week without walking into anything around him. I sit quietly for the rest of the trip while Sawyer and Jared catch up. Sawyer seems to make friends wherever she goes and somehow stays on good terms and in touch with all of them. She met Jared while protesting against whaling one summer with an environmental group off Japan. His mother is a marine biologist, and he had been along for the adventure.

They became fast friends and had stayed in touch ever since. Jared only spent summers growing up with his mom, living the rest of the year inland in Colorado. He and Caleb are both snowboarders. Caleb competed the year before but had had a nasty fall and fractured his wrist. Jared isn't very competitive, he mainly boards for fun and works just enough to have plenty of time for it.

He says dude a lot, starting almost every third sentence with it. Out of curiosity, I start mentally counting them to see how many times he'll say it between now and their apartment. I count to thirty-two, I think, as he pulls into a parking spot. In that moment, I'm pretty sure I won't be falling in love with Jared.

He and Caleb live on the ground floor. He carries our bags as we follow him into his apartment.

Caleb is sitting on the sofa, his wrist in a cast. He stands to hug both of us, his hug for Sawyer noticeably longer than mine. This is not their first meeting. Caleb is originally from Minnesota and Jared put Sawyer in touch with him once when she was in St Paul. She had been tagging along with some friends who were in a band. Tired of the VW Bus she had been crammed in, she crashed with Caleb for a weekend. I never got the entire story out of her on what they did that weekend, but I had a good idea. When he sat back down, she sat next to him and fingered his cast as she asked how his recovery was going.

I follow Jared into the kitchen after he says, "Dude, I could go for a beer. Want one, Sarah?"

I could absolutely use a beer, but I hesitate when he hands me a Miller Lite. He gives me a look, and I grab it before he thinks that maybe I don't like the brand. It just reminds me of Will. Being reminded of Will in the presence of the dude-spouting potential replacement is not a good thing. All it does is drive home how not Will Jared is. His strikes are adding up. Now that we are inside, I'm able to check him out without his hat or bulky coat on. He has short, almost buzzed dark brown hair and is built. I find myself staring at his chest and suddenly don't mind his overuse of the word dude.

Since I have a meeting the next day, we all just hang out that night and watch a movie. Sawyer and Caleb disappear halfway through, which makes things a little awkward with me and Jared, especially after the movie is unable to drown out the, um, noises they're making. At first, we both try to pretend like neither of us can hear them. Then I can't hold it in any longer. I giggle. Thankfully, that seems to break the tension, for a short while anyway. Jared laughs. I laugh. Then we just look at each other, and it's awkward all over again.

Sawyer and I are supposed to be sharing the pull out sofa this week. Clearly, it's all mine now. I just can't actually go to sleep until Jared gets off of it. I really do need to get a good night's sleep but don't have it in me to point blank tell him that. Instead, I yawn, even though I'm not really that tired, and then I yawn again. That doesn't seem to work. Finally, twenty dudes later, I ask him if I can use his bathroom to get ready for bed. Their apartment is a double master with the living room and kitchen between the two bedrooms, and each bedroom has its bathroom. It's a cool set up but lacks a standalone guest bathroom.

I grabbed my PJs and toiletry bag and follow Jared into his room. Very awkward. His room is cool, though. He has boards all over the place. Some are leaned up against the far corner of his room. Others are mounted on the wall above his bed and over his dresser. Seeing them like that, it strikes me that they're not unlike art. His room is neat even though his bed isn't made. It smells nice, like aftershave, and it's faint, but I swear I can smell Febreeze. Jared walks me to the bathroom door and points out where the spare towels are before leaving me so he can set up the pull out.

His bathroom is also clean for a boy. I laugh when I see how much hair product he has, considering his hair is so short. I go ahead and take a shower since I'm kind of nervous about access to the bathroom the next morning. I'm just stepping out of the shower when I hear a knock on the door. I hurriedly pull on my PJs and crack the door.

"Everything okay?" I ask.

"Dude, the shower head leaks unless you jiggle the knob. You can't hear it with the fan on. I wanted to show you what to do before I forgot."

I open the door and step further into the bathroom to make room for him. He demonstrates proper knob jiggling.

"Why don't you have maintenance fix it?" I ask when he's done.

"Oh, I gave up on them. They've been up here a bunch of times. Once I figured out how to make it stop on my own, I figured it was pointless to call them again."

"That makes sense," I concede, brushing my hair.

I inhale when Jared leans over and smells my hair. He straightens and shrugs. "I like the way your hair smells."

I blush. "Um, thanks. I'm just going to brush my teeth and go to bed if that's cool."

Jared nods and walks out into his bedroom. He doesn't shut the door behind him, so I brush my teeth quickly and follow him.

"So tomorrow are you still able to give me a lift to my meeting? It's on the early side, and I don't want to put you out. You're already letting Sawyer and me crash here, which is so cool of you."

"Dude, it's my pleasure. What time do you want me to wake you up? I can set my alarm."

After we're clear on all the details, I get settled in the living room. As I drift off to sleep, I wonder what my problem is. Jared is a super hot guy, who I think might be into me, but I just can't stop thinking about Will.

~*~

My meeting goes amazingly. I had spent a lot of time preparing my proposal, and I think it paid off. They seem really interested in my ideas and the services I'm able to offer. The coolest part of my job is working with small business owners. They are so passionate about what they do every day and figuring out employee-sponsored plans is usually not something they want to think about. In fact, most of the time, it scares them, and I love to see the look in their eyes when they realize I can take all of that stress away and free up their time to do what they started their business for in the first place. Growing up, I never thought this would be my dream job, but I loved helping people and knowing what I'm doing makes me feel really good about myself.

Jared is in his Tahoe waiting for me outside the office building where my meeting was. My ear to ear grin clued him in that the meeting went well so he took me out to lunch to celebrate. I try telling him that even though the meeting went well there was no guarantee that they would actually hire me. It is only fifteen minutes after I said that when they call me. I feel rude for taking the call while Jared and I were at lunch but Jared told me I was crazy and to answer the phone. My mouth drops open when they tell me they loved my proposal and wanted to hire me. Since they were able to decide so quickly there was a chance I would be able to get all of their paperwork together that week.

When I hang up with them, Jared walks over to my side of the booth and gives me a hug. I start crying, which makes him nervous. I have to tell him ten times they're happy tears before he believes me. Why am I not attracted to him? He's cute and sweet and smells good. I could do way worse. Jared laughs at me the whole ride back to his apartment as I happy dance in my seat. I cannot wait to tell Sawyer how my meeting went and that they have already hired me. That has never happened on the same day I give my presentation. Sawyer and Caleb are eating nachos in the living room when we get back, her legs in his lap.

There's a close call with a plate of nachos that Caleb manages to catch with his good hand as Sawyer jumps up to hug me. She wants us to all go out tonight and celebrate, but I put her off until the next night because I still have another meeting the next day. Once the initial rush of adrenaline wears off, I manage to corner Sawyer in the kitchen.

"Not cool last night. Just saying."

She hugs me. "I'm so sorry we ditched you guys like that. Did anything happen with you and Jared?"

"No, I just. I don't know," I mumble.

She makes a face at me. "Sarah, Jared is one of the good guys. I've known him a really long time."

I groan. "I know. He's hot and he's been really sweet to me. I even get the feeling that he might be interested in me. I can't explain it." I don't tell her about the dude thing because it sounds shallow. The rest of the day is low key. I don't even bat an eye when Sawyer and Caleb head into his room even earlier than they did the last night. I grab my things to get ready for bed and dash into Jared's bathroom before he has a chance to say anything to me. I want to avoid any uncomfortable silences and contemplate strangling Sawyer the next time I see her.

Jared has the pull out all made up by the time I'm finished. He lingers by his bedroom door for a minute like he wants to say something but doesn't. Part of me wishes I was interested in him. He seems like a nice guy, and he's hot. Life sucks that way. You don't get to choose who you fall for.

~*~

A gentle shake of my shoulder wakes me. I open one eye and see Jared leaning over me.

"Coffee?" he asks.

I can smell the mouthwash on his breath and clamp my lips together and nod before heading to his bathroom. I brush my teeth before I come back out. A mug is waiting for me on their breakfast bar. I'm not sure why, but since yesterday's meeting went so well, I feel even more nervous about my meeting today. It's like I won't feel like I've done a good job unless I have a similar result today. Jared makes us his own version of an egg McMuffin using this microwavable plastic egg cooker and English muffins. He eats three to my one, and he flicks bread crumbs at me when I laugh at him. I can definitely see us becoming friends.

On the way to the office building where my next meeting is, I start panicking and ask Jared to pull over so I can get out of the car. He probably thinks I'm crazy, but he doesn't hesitate and I feel better after getting out and taking a few breaths. Once we're on the road again, I feel more confident. Jared waits for me again outside the building. I catch myself thinking about how nice that is while I sit in the waiting room of the dentist I'm meeting. My meeting goes well. Dr. Larsen is very methodical so I can already tell I won't be getting the almost instant result I had the day before. He does say that he'll be in touch three times, which I take as a good sign as I walk out.

Jared treats me to lunch again on the way back. While we eat, he tells me more about himself and living in Colorado. One day of our trip, Jared and Caleb are taking us snowboarding at Loveland. When he goes by himself, he prefers Breckenridge or Eldora, but since Sawyer and I are both beginners, Loveland is closer to where they live and less overwhelming. When we get back to their apartment, Caleb is drinking coffee, and Sawyer is still asleep. I think about going in and waking her but stop myself, not wanting to find out if she's naked. I change out of my work clothes and into a pair of jeans and a sweater. We're watching TV when she joins us, yawning and stretching the whole way before settling in Caleb's lap. Sawyer has an almost cat like quality to her. She never walks. She slinks. The cotton candy toned streaks in her hair are long gone, replaced with a vibrant red tone and black low lights.

She yawns again before looking over at me and grinning. "Now that all that work stuff is out of the way, we are so going clubbing tonight."

I wrinkle my nose. Clubbing? That's always more her thing than mine, and I'm not sure if I had even packed anything dressy enough.

She reads my mind. She has a way of doing that. "I have the perfect dress for you."

Chapter 25

Present

I wake in Will's arms. The only time that has ever happened before is that day in the lounge chair by his parents' pool. I think back to last night, his mouth on me and then my tears. I can't really explain why I cried. I'm only embarrassed that I did. I move to slip out of his grasp, only to feel his grip tighten.

"You're not getting away this time, Sarah," he murmurs in my ear.

"Aww. That's sweet and all, but unless you're into golden showers you're going to wanna let me go to the bathroom."

He squeezes tighter.

"Will, if you make me pee in my big brother's bed I will never forgive you."

"Where's the romance?" he grumbles, releasing me.

"That kind of romance is only in movies, where people never use the bathroom or have morning breath," I shout, streaking to the bathroom.

I'm heading back to the room now clad in a towel when I hear noise in the kitchen. I bite back a laugh when I see Will leaning over the kitchen sink, in his boxers, brushing his teeth.

He shrugs at my expression. I walk up behind him, wrapping my arms around his waist and lean on him. His back feels warm against my cheek. He rinses his mouth before turning to face me, his lips finding mine. A minty fresh tongue dips into my mouth, and I'm thankful I brushed my teeth while I was in the bathroom. His hands relieve me of my towel, and he lifts me onto their kitchen island.

"This can't be sanitary," I tease as he comes to stand between my legs.

In the morning light from the balcony door, I'm able to fully appreciate how much his body has changed since we were kids. He stills when my hands move to the waistband of his boxers. I know what he's thinking. I had said no sex, but last night changed something in me. If Will will have me, I know I will find any way to be in his life again.

"I want you inside me," I plead.

"I don't have any condoms."

"I have an implant."

"Do what?" He pulls back, looking at me.

"It's birth control implanted in my arm." I raise my arm and point to where it's inserted.

"Why?"

"Don't laugh."

He gives me a look.

"Okay. So Sawyer, my best friend, is very much a free spirit. She could never remember to take the pill and had a couple of pregnancy scares. She needed a more long term solution but was too scared to do it by herself, so being a good friend and not wanting to ever have to read another pregnancy exam to her ever, I agreed to get one with her so she wouldn't be alone."

His finger traces the edge of the implant, his eyes intense. "So what you're saying," his hand moving between my thighs, "is we can be very spontaneous?"

I nod, my breath catching. His lips crush mine as I tangle my fingers in his hair. Will lifts me, my legs wrapping around his waist, and carries me back to the bedroom. He lays me onto the bed, covering me, grinding his hips against mine. I moan, and he's gone. My eyes flutter open, and I watch as he takes off his boxers.

"Are you sure?" he asks as he lies back down with me.

I nod, my hands reaching for him.

His lips are on my neck. "I want to hear you say it."

I groan and lift his chin until his eyes meet mine. "Yes, I'm sure."

His lips cut off anything else I'm about to say, and he slowly eases into me. His lips never stray far from mine as our bodies move together. If there was ever a doubt in my mind, it is gone now. I'm made for him, and he's made for me. There will never be anything else for either of us.

Now spent, we cling to each other. Will can't stop kissing me and trails his lips over the side of my face, lifting his head to look at me when I smile.

I giggle. "Will, we just did it."

He grins. "God, I love you."

My face falls as I bury my face in his chest.

His finger under my chin, he lifts my face to his. "Sarah, what's wrong?"

I pull my lips into my mouth and bite them, my eyes watering. I shake my head.

"Please tell me," he pleads, his eyes wide.

I sniffle and close my eyes, trying not to cry. "I'm so sorry I left. I'm so sorry I did that to you. Please believe me."

He puts his hands on either side of my face and gently kisses me. "Don't cry." Another kiss. "Please don't cry." Another kiss. "Please look at me." Another kiss. "We were so young." Another kiss. My eyes open to look into his wet ones. "You didn't know." Another kiss. "We can't change the past." Another kiss. "We're together now." Another kiss. "I just want to make you happy."

Tears stream down the sides of my face. Will looks panicked, and I pull his lips to mine. "I love you so much." Another kiss. "You make me happier than I have ever been." Another kiss.

"Why are you crying?"

"I don't know. I feel like an emotional wreck. Are you sure you want all of this?"

He brushes a tear from my cheek. "There is nothing I have ever wanted more."

We kiss and hold each other until our empty stomachs protest. Wearing Will's undershirt, I blush when I see the kitchen island. As Will starts the coffee maker, I discretely wipe down the island top. I see him watching me out of the corner of his eye, and I walk up behind him to lean on him. He's wearing his boxers. My arms wrap around his waist, and he puts his arms over them, holding me in an embrace. I rest my cheek on his shoulder blade and listen to his heart beat. He lifts one hand from mine and opens the cabinet above the coffee maker.

"Frosted Mini Wheats or Lucky Charms?"

"Are you sure they have milk?" I ask, hopeful.

He turns, and I move with him so he can open the fridge. He hums as he reads the expiration date.

"Just enough for two bowls and not expired."

I kiss his back before reaching around him to grab the Lucky Charms. He turns to face me and grins as I now hug the cereal box.

"Gonna share?"

I give the box a shake to try and gauge how full it is before nodding. Will leans down to kiss me before getting a couple of bowls down from another cabinet. Each with our bowl in hand, we walk into the living room and eat curled up on the sofa. Will flips the TV on to a local station. Just like old times, Will is finished before me, his bowl sitting empty by his feet. His hand is on my leg, and I have to remind myself to eat. It's hard though, knowing that he's watching me. Finally, he turns his attention towards the TV after I give him a look. His hand still on my leg proves to be too much of a distraction for me. I set my half eaten cereal on the coffee table and look at him. He's tan and cut. I reach out and touch his stomach, smiling when he inhales sharply and looks at me.

"Do you workout?" I ask, curious.

He snakes an arm around my waist and pulls me into his lap. "Like what you see?"

I roll my eyes at him and laugh. "Dork. It was just a question. You clearly know you look good."

He drops his lips to my neck. "I try and swim laps a few times a week and play basketball."

"No lacrosse?"

He shakes his head. "There really isn't anything to do around here. I goof around at home, that's all. What about you?"

I wrinkle my nose. "I travel so much. Does running through airports count?" He shakes his head. "I drink a lot of water and do some yoga. Really just basic stuff. My balance is crap. It would probably get better if I tried harder, but..." I lay my head on his chest.

"Whatever you are doing is working so don't change a thing." He rests his chin on my head.

I bring my hand up to his chest and trace the contours of his chest with my finger. Will truly has a beautiful body, strong and firm. I could touch him all day. His arms tighten around me, and his head dips so his lips can find my neck. We make our way back to the spare bedroom. Will almost steps on his empty bowl when he lifts me from the couch.

"I can walk, you know," I tease, kissing his neck.

"This is more romantic."

"Oh, alright. Carry on then."

~*~

Much later, after a shower, Will asks me to go with him to speak to his mother. I own my own business, a successful one, and I'm twenty-five years old. Why do I feel so nervous about what she will think of me? Will and I talk on the way about possible flight plans. How soon he comes to join me somewhat depends on how well our conversation with his mother goes. I can't help but remember the last time I was at his house when we pull up. It was senior skip day, and we had fallen asleep by the pool. I wonder if she ever would have said those things to me on the phone if she had not found us that way that day.

Will leans over to kiss me before we walk up together. He takes my hand in his as we enter his house. His mother is in the living room. Will says hello, but she doesn't respond. She just turns her head and acknowledges his presence. Her gaze stops and rests on our joined hands before moving up to look at my face. If she recognizes me, she doesn't show it. Will leads further into the room, and we sit, side by side on the sofa, facing the armchair she is sitting in. The house is still exactly as it was when I was here the last time. A living museum to the dead.

"Mom." She looks over at him. "Do you remember my friend, Sarah Miller?"

Her eyes snap to my face and widen briefly before dropping to our still joined hands. She nods.

Will chews on the side of his lip before going on. "Sarah lives in Colorado now, and since I'm on summer break, I'd like to go out and visit her. Do you think that would be alright?"

She doesn't do anything immediately, but after a moment, her face crumbles, and she lifts her hands to cover her face. Will releases my hand and goes to kneel by her, gently shushing her and rubbing her back. She leans into him and grips his shoulders as she cries. I sit uncomfortably on the sofa, not sure what to do. Any hope of her support in the trip seems in vain. Will manages to get her to calm down, and I go with him up to his room so he can change. He sees the anxiety in my eyes and pulls me to him once his door is shut. It seemed like such a fantasy, us coming together the way that we did, after all of these years.

"Have you left her by herself before?"

Will chews the side of his lip. "Nothing longer than a night here and there since my dad died."

"She just doesn't leave the house?"

He nods. "Not since she came back from the hospital that day."

"But she takes care of herself otherwise?"

"She doesn't cook anymore but will eat things that are already prepared. I keep the kitchen stocked with ready made stuff."

"What do you want to do?"

He brings one hand up to scratch the back of his head. "Ideally, maybe hire someone to stay with her while I'm gone."

I frown. "Do you know anyone?"

He shakes his head, and I sink onto his bed. I leave tomorrow. It seems clear that Will won't be able to come with me, at least right away. He changes out of his dress pants and shirt and into cargo shorts that sit on his hips in a way that makes my mouth water. He catches my eye as he pulls a t-shirt over his head.

"I'm going to go check on her again. I'll be right back." He leans down and kisses me before leaving me in his room.

I stand and walk around his room. This is the first time I've ever been in his bedroom. I wonder if it's changed much from when we were in school. The rest of the house looks exactly the same from the last time I saw it. I sit back down on his bed and take out my phone. I need to talk to Sawyer.

I exhale when she answers.

"What's up, buttercup?"

"So Will and I happened last night, and this morning," I say, spinning my ring.

"Whoa. Are we happy or sad about this?"

"Happy, definitely happy. Maybe a bit freaked out too."

"Freaked out is acceptable."

"He mentioned coming home with me, but his mom has issues so he's going to need to find someone to stay with her, and who knows how long something like that will take. I'm just scared that once there's space between us he'll change his mind."

"What's the deal with his mom?"

"I think I told you how she got after Will's sister died, right?"

"Mm hmm."

"I guess she got even worse after his dad died. She won't leave the house or cook, and she lost it when

Will mentioned spending the rest of the summer with me."

"She still showers herself and gets dressed though, right?"

I laugh. I'm not sure why. "I think so. She's dressed right now and looks showered. Will didn't say that was something he did for her when we talked about it."

"I can do it."

I pull my phone away for a moment and look at her contact icon before answering. "Do what?"

"I can mamasit. That way it won't take forever to find someone, and you guys can have the place all to yourselves."

"Sawyer, that's crazy. His mom probably needs a professional. I don't think Will would go for it."

"Just putting it out there."

"Who knows? I'll mention it to him."

"So back to this Will fella. Did he rock your socks off?"

I blush. "Last night, he went down on me, and I cried. How embarrassing is that? Full on ugly cry."

"And he didn't ditch you last night?" she jokes.

"He has a tattoo about me too."

"Shut up. That's hot. What is it?"

"A Miller Lite logo on his chest."

She laughs. "Are you sure he just doesn't like girl beer?"

"No, he used to always call me that. It was like his name for me." I look up when Will walks back into his room. "Hang on a sec, Sawyer." I hold my phone to my shoulder. "Will, Sawyer offered to come stay with your mom."

"Can I talk to her?" he asks, holding out his hand for the phone.

I put the phone back to my ear. "Will wants to talk to you," I tell her before handing the phone to him.

I sit and watch as he paces back and forth in front of me. Sawyer seems to be asking questions about his mom that he is answering. Every so often, he looks over at me and either shrugs or smiles. After five minutes, I lie back on his bed and soak in his scent. If he can't leave with me tomorrow I may ask for his pillow. Their conversation seems to go well. He hangs up the phone and jumps on me.

I laugh, pushing him onto his side. "So what'd you guys decide?"

"I've got a flight to book," he says before lifting his mouth to mine.

I melt into his kiss before pulling back. "Really?"

"Yep." He kisses me again. "I should probably start packing." He rolls onto me. "But there's something I have to do first." His hands move to the waistband of my jeans.

"Will," I gasp. "Your mom."

"Shhh, you don't want her to hear you, do you?" He silences me with his lips.

We're in high school all over again. My jeans dangle from one leg, and his shorts are pushed down only just past his knees as he enters me. We're frantic, my hands pulling him closer and faster to me. He's on my elbows. His hands are in my hair. I crash first, Will just after me. We're both panting as his eyes meet mine. I brush his hair off of his forehead and giggle. We're both still dressed from the waist up.

"I'm liking spontaneous," he grins before lowering his lips to mine.

We both still when we hear a noise from downstairs and quickly get dressed. I dash to the bathroom across the hall and freshen up. My hair is a mess. I use what I assume is Will's comb to get out any tangles and pull it up in a ponytail. Will is packing when I walk back into his room.

"You are so bad," I tease, closing the door behind me.

He leaves his suitcase on the bed and pins me against the door. "I just can't seem to help myself."

I'm breathless as he nibbles on my earlobe. He lifts me, his hands gripping me, and I wrap my legs around his waist. He walks me over to his bed and sets me down.

"You're making packing hard," he grumbles before straightening and taking a step back from me.

"I'm not doing anything," I argue, shaking my head. I look down at his suitcase. "Are you cool with Sawyer staying with your mom? You've never even met her."

He's taking a dress shirt off of a hanger. "She seems like a trip, but she's your best friend. That's all I need to know."

"So when will she get here?"

"Her flight lands midnight."

My mouth drops open. "Tonight?"

He nods, folding the shirt and setting it in his suitcase.

"And she got me a seat on your flight tomorrow."

I blink away the tears that are threatening me. "So you're really coming back with me?"

Will takes in my expression and comes to stand in front of me, pulling me into his arms. "I'm not losing you again."

Chapter 26

Past

The dress Sawyer has for me will never fit. I'm a good four inches taller than her. I somehow manage to get the dress on, but it's so tight in the shoulders I can barely lift or move my arms.

"It looks great," Sawyer gushes.

I give her a look and try and lift my arms. "I feel like a T-Rex. There is no way I can dance in this."

"A T-REX!" She bends over, clutching her stomach as she laughs.

"What am I going to wear?"

She holds up her hand as she keeps laughing. After a few moments she looks up. "We'll just have to go shopping now, won't we?"

"Sawyer, I can't afford to spend any money right now."

"Hush, silly. I'm the one who wants to go out. It's my treat."

Sawyer and I have been friends for almost five years now. I don't know the whole story, but Sawyer lives off of a trust fund. I don't know how much is in it or how she got it, and I usually don't let her buy me things. I make an exception this time after I make her promise it will just be an early birthday present. Like three months early. She gets Jared to drive us to the mall, and I let her drag me into Forever 21. I sit with Jared as Sawyer buzzes around the store, grabbing different outfits for me to try on. I can only take eight items back at a time, so she sets the rest of the clothes she's accumulated in my now empty chair and sits on the armrest of Jared's chair while I go try them on.

A couple of the dresses I refuse to show them. One is just way too low cut in the front, and I feel uncomfortable in it. The other is cute but too tight in the top, and I can't move my arms in it either. When I show them the next outfit, I take out the second dress to see if Sawyer can find it one size up. The fourth outfit I try on is my favorite so far, a stretchy charcoal pencil skirt and a striped tank top. Sawyer starts complaining that she wanted the gray skirt to go with some see-through top and the striped tank to go with a sequined micro mini. I laugh at her because there is no way I'll wear either of those combos.

She grumbles about my lack of fashion sense and stalks off in search of that dress in a larger size.

"I like what you're wearing." Jared smiles up at me.

"Apparently, I'm not showing enough skin."

He shakes his head. "Let her pick out crazy shoes for you, and she'll be fine."

I laugh. He's right, and he knows it. It makes me wonder how many times Sawyer has dragged him out shopping over the years. When she comes back, I take his advice and end up with the outfit I like and a pair of hot pink cowboy boots. We pick up dinner on the way home and hang out around the coffee table to eat. Caleb joins us a few minutes later, squeezing in between Sawyer and me on the couch.

"What'd the doctor say?" Jared asks.

"Might be able to get the cast off a week early."

Sawyer makes a face. "Bummer they couldn't take it off today."

Caleb laughs and pulls her towards him for a kiss. "You can barely handle me one handed."

Her mouth drops, and she smacks his stomach. "You're lucky you're cute."

"Just cute?" he asks in mock horror.

She rolls her eyes and eats a French fry.

After dinner, we get ready in Caleb's room and bathroom while Jared and Caleb watch TV. Sawyer flat irons her hair, and I curl mine. I let her do my makeup and mentally remind myself to wash my face before I go to bed today so I don't end up looking like a raccoon in the morning. Sawyer ended up buying the silver sequined mini and paired it with a black tank and boots. We do a couple of shots with Caleb before putting on our coats and heading out. There's a coat check at the club so we don't have to worry about finding a place to stash our winter coats.

Sawyer pulls me right out onto the dance floor, Jared and Caleb following us. Sawyer and Caleb basically make out the whole time while Jared and I dance. He's a good dancer, and the music is so loud there we can't really talk. He stands behind me, hands on my hips, my back to his chest. He doesn't try and feel me up, and since he's there, no one else tries to dance with me. I like him. I do, just as a friend. After a few songs, we stop to all get drinks and cool off. When we're standing at the bar, a guy asks me if I want to dance. Jared stops him and says I'm with him.

After that guy leaves, I ask him about it.

"Sorry. That guy's a tool, but there are some cool guys here if you want me to introduce you to any of them."

I smile. "No, that's okay. I was just curious."

"You're a nice girl, Sarah."

"Thanks. Where'd that come from?"

"I love Sawyer, but she's crazy. I didn't know what to expect from you."

"I can be a little crazy," I joke and take a sip of my drink.

"Nah, you're a cool chick. Seeing you all excited after your meetings was cool."

I blush. I was practically jumping up and down after my first meeting.

"Sawyer needs a friend like you." He looks over at her making out with Caleb. "Someone with common sense."

"I don't know if I have—"

He cuts me off. "You do. Trust me."

We finish our drinks and dance some more. After that, Jared introduces me to some people he knows. We all end up leaving the club and going over to one of their houses. It's a beautiful craftsman-style home. It's too dark out to tell, but I have a feeling it has some sweet mountain views. Everyone is hanging out in the finished basement. Someone breaks out a joint, and it's passed around the room. I decline, and Jared grins at me, surprising me by also passing. I kinda figured he was a pothead.

"You don't smoke?"

He shakes his head. "Makes me lazy."

I laugh. I've only gotten high a couple of times. "I get hungry and paranoid. Not fun."

"Want to play pool?"

He racks the balls, and I break. .We both laugh at how little the balls move. Jared sets them back up and makes me go again. This try is better. A couple of balls go in, and I call solids.

~*~

The next morning, I cringe when I look in the mirror. Yep. Forgot to wash my face last night, or more accurately, this morning when we got home from the party. We were all so tired I didn't even wait for Jared to fold out the bed, just crashed on the sofa instead. I normally wait for Jared to get up before I use his bathroom, but I really have to go. It feels weird walking past him as he sleeps. I jump when I hear him knock on the door. I dry my face and open the door.

"Hey, can I?" Jared motions into the bathroom.

"Of course." I move past him and back into the living room.

I'm making a pot of coffee when he comes out of his room. I laugh at how bleary-eyed he looks, and he shrugs. It's funny how much Jared reminds me of Brian. He just has this easy-going way about him. Ever since he offered to introduce me to guys, I've felt more comfortable around him. Not that I want to meet guys, but he wouldn't have made that offer if he was interested in me. It'd be nice to have a guy friend again, and I can see him being that for me. We have our coffee and eat breakfast. Neither of us are shocked that Sawyer and Caleb don't make it out of Caleb's room until two hours later. We're watching a reality TV marathon on MTV.

"Those cats are mental," Caleb says, looking at the TV.

"But entertaining." I grin.

"Fair enough," he says, sitting down.

Jared gets up to get a drink. "Anyone want to go tubing tonight?"

"Like sledding?" I ask.

"Exactly. They've got a night run like thirty minutes from here."

"I'm game," Sawyer says from the kitchen.

"Still want to go boarding tomorrow too, right?"

I nod while Sawyer says. "Hell yeah."

Caleb sits on the couch, looking at his cast. Sawyer sees his pout and sits in his lap.

"Can you go tubing?" she asks.

He nods and laughs as she shimmies in his lap and says, "SWEET!"

After we all eat lunch, I borrow Jared's laptop to email documents to the couple from the first day. They run a wellness center, focusing on helping people find balance. They offer mainly yoga-based fitness classes, diet counseling, and meditation clinics. They have a staff of ten part-time and full-time employees and are setting up individual 401Ks for each. I use a draft file in my email to save all the documents I use on a regular basis. I email them everything they need to set up their accounts. They're going to use a managed service with a wire house to manage the investment options for the relationship. Each employee will have the ultimate decision in what funds they select for their individual account.

I send the email with times that I'll be available to come in the day before our flight leaves. One unique service I provide is being there in person for all of the paperwork. These plans can be complex and overwhelming. It's my job to make that process as smooth and stress free as possible. If they're able to meet with me before I leave, I won't have to deal with booking another flight out. Any savings I can manage just increase my profit. I'm supporting myself, which I'm really proud of considering I'm my own boss, but I'm not raking in excess cash either.

Caleb and Jared leave to go pick up a new board Jared had ordered from a local board shop. Sawyer and I stay back. I feel like I've barely had a chance to talk to her alone the whole time we've been in Colorado.

"So things seem to be going well with Caleb."

Sawyer blushes. She never blushes. "Things are amazing with Caleb."

"That's great," I say, giving her a hug.

"I know. I actually wanted to run something by you." She hesitates.

"Okay?" I push her knee.

"I'm thinking about moving out here, and I want you to come with me."

My mouth drops open.

"I know it sounds crazy, Sarah, but think about it. What is keeping us in Trenton? Your uncle moved to Florida last year, and you had two really good meetings here."

"I don't know," I stammer.

She stands and starts pacing back and forth in front of me, counting off on her fingers all of the reasons she thinks we should move out here.

I laugh when wanting to see what Caleb can do with both hands makes the list and argue. "That reason has zero impact for me."

"True, but I know for a fact Jared likes you so that can be your romance reason."

I groan. "Sawyer, Jared is hot. I get that. And he seems like a really nice guy, but I don't like him that way."

Her brows push together. "Is it because of Will?"

I let my head fall back onto the sofa and look up at the ceiling. I hate how shaky my voice sounds when I say, "He's just a tough act to follow, I guess."

She comes to sit next to me and shakes my knee. I turn my head to look at her, my eyes wet.

"Maybe if you live someplace new, someplace you didn't run away to, you will get over him."

She does have a point there. It's been over four years since I had moved to New Jersey, but even now if I drive past the train station or Jake's old apartment, I think back to the day I ran away. Sawyer's right. Now that my uncle lives in Florida, there's nothing keeping me in Trenton.

I close my eyes and take a deep breath. "Let's do it."

She grabs both of my shoulders and gets right in my face, almost nose to nose. "Really?"

I nod.

She pulls me forward into a bear hug as she jumps up and down on the sofa. I laugh and push her off of me. She gets up and happy dances in front of the coffee table. I'm shaking my head, watching her when Caleb and Jared walk back in. Jared looks at me, and I shrug. I can't explain the crazy that is Sawyer. She sees Caleb behind him, grabs his hand, and she pulls him into his room, shutting the door behind them.

"What was that all about?" Jared asks, carrying his new board into his room.

I get up and follow him. "I think we're moving to Colorado."

His back is to me as he leans his new board in the corner of his room. He pauses before turning to face me. He's grinning, and I yelp when he pulls me into a hug. Maybe if I live here and get to know him better, I can like Jared as more than a friend. For now, I still need time. My body tenses in his arms. I cringe when he notices and drops his arms.

He takes a step back from me and scratches the back of his head. "That's cool."

"I'm not sure when, or how, or where we'll live. We just talked about it right before you and Caleb got back," I ramble.

Jared sits on the edge of his bed. "Relax, Sarah. Let Sawyer figure all of that stuff out. That girl is an expert at moving."

He motions for me to sit down, patting the spot next to him on the bed. I shrug and sit down next to him. He turns his body towards mine, motioning with his finger for me to turn my back to him.

"Why are you so tense?" he asks, his hands rubbing my shoulders.

"Don't know," I mumble.

I sit quietly as he massages my neck and shoulders but tense when his hands move further down my back. I roll my eyes when I hear him chuckling behind me.

"What?" I turn my head.

"You are like one giant knot."

"Why's that funny?"

"It isn't, but the ways I was thinking about getting you to chill out were."

I hunch my shoulders, which makes him laugh even more.

"Fine," I snap. "How would you get me to relax?"

"Hot tub."

"But it's freezing outside," I stammer.

"Our complex has an indoor pool and hot tub."

"Oh, doesn't matter. I didn't bring a suit."

He tugs on my bra strap through my shirt. "Wear this."

I think about it for a moment. "Any other ideas?"

"You could wear nothing."

"Ha! You're funny. I meant any ideas other than the hot tub."

He takes his hands off my back and lies back on his bed. "I don't see you going for any of my other ideas. Besides, after we go tubing tonight, you'll be all for chilling out in the hot tub. If you're worried about not having a suit, I can run you over to the mall right now."

I stand, stretching my arms up over my head. My muscles do feel more relaxed. "Thanks for the shoulder rub. You don't have to take me anywhere. I'll be fine with stuff I brought."

I turn to walk out of his room, and he calls out for me to stop.

I look back at him. "Yeah?"

"You can hang out with me in here."

I look around. There isn't really anywhere to sit besides his bed. "You look like you're about to take a nap."

He yawns. "Dude, late night last night. Aren't you tired?"

I am. I'm thinking about curling up on the sofa myself. "I am."

"Why don't you lay down in here?"

He laughs at the expression on my face. "No pressure. I'll keep my hands to myself. That couch is uncomfortable. You could sleep in here."

"With you?"

"Just sleep, Sarah."

I wrinkle my nose. "I don't know."

He gets up and tugs me back over to the bed. "Look, Sarah. I think you're cute. I'd like to be your friend. I won't try anything."

I lie down, facing the ceiling. He walks into the living room and grabs the blanket I have been using and covers me with it. I yawn and turn onto my side. He lies down next to me, leaving plenty of space between us, and closes his eyes. I look at him for a little bit before I fall asleep. The last thing I remember thinking is if I'll feel something for someone other than Will.

Chapter 27

Present

Will's hand is on my leg as we drive to the airport. Once he was done packing, we got the guest bedroom of his house all set for Sawyer before he spoke with his mother again. I waited in his car while he explained to her Sawyer was coming to stay with her for the time he would be with me in Colorado. He had made her dinner after he talked to her, and then we went to my parents' house to have dinner with them and my uncle Chip. My parents were thrilled Will and I are together. It was strange, but since they see him more than me, it felt like they were happier for him. It's like they all know how important this is to him. My uncle had pulled me aside after dinner. He's the only member of my family who knows how messed up I was over Will the last time.

He was cautiously happy for us. He just didn't want to ever see me hurt again. I had smacked his arm when he joked he had a spare bedroom in Florida if I ever needed it. Running had been my M.O. when it came to Will for so long. I'm scared by how fast everything is happening but also recognize that while it feels fast it has also been a long time coming. It feels like we're meant to be together. If we weren't, one of us would have moved on by now. I put my hand on top of his and squeeze it. His eyes flick to mine, and he smiles. I know he's stressed out over this whole thing with his mom. He wants to be angry at her for the part she played in my leaving, but she's his mom. I respect that about him. Will is the type of guy that does the right thing no matter what the situation.

We check the arrivals display once we're in the airport. Sawyer's flight had landed ahead of schedule so we hurry over to baggage claim to look for her. I spot her cotton candy pink hair from across the floor and run over to hug her.

"Hey, babe." She laughs, dropping her bag to hug me back.

I pull away to look at her. "Thank you so much for this. I just…" I can't finish without crying.

"Please, it's nothing." She pauses and squints at me. "Getting laid looks good on you, babe."

I blush and shush her as Will walks up to us. Her mouth drops when she gets a good look at him.

He holds out his hand, and she pushes it away and gives him a hug instead.

When he isn't looking, she mouths, "He's hot" at me.

Will looks at me when I laugh so I stick my tongue out at him and grin.

Sawyer lets Will carry her bags and links her arm through mine as we walk to his car. "I'm not sure if I've ever seen you look this happy, Sarah."

I shrug and look back at Will to see if he heard her. He meets my eyes and winks at me, grinning. I offer the front seat to Sawyer, but she refuses and climbs into the backseat.

"Before I forget, here's my parking ticket," she says, passing me a slip of paper. Since Will and I will be arriving the next day in Colorado, she had just driven to the airport and left her car there. That way, we can just use her car instead of getting a cab. The cost of overnight parking isn't that bad.

Sawyer grills Will about us and his mother most of the way back to his house. I freeze when she asks a question I have always wanted to know the answer to.

"Why didn't you go after Sarah when she went to New Jersey?"

He glances over at me when he feels me tense under his hand. "I did."

My mouth drops. "What?"

He nods, eyes on the road. "I was a wreck after you left. My dad almost canceled the trip to Italy, but my mom talked him out of it. I barely remember the trip. I was in this fog of worrying about what happened to you." His fingers tighten on the wheel. "You just disappeared, and Brian wouldn't tell me right away where you went. I didn't even know you went to your uncle's until after I got back. The day I found out, I drove up there. I had to stop and stay in a shitty motel on the way 'cause there was construction happening on some bridge, and it took forever to get over it. I just couldn't wait to see you, to hold you, to bring you back with me. I didn't know why you left, but I knew I could get you to come back. When I got to your uncle's place, no one was home. I just sat in my car and waited for like two hours. I was just thinking about driving to get some food when I saw you pull up with some guy in a truck." He pauses, chewing his lip before going on. "You were laughing. You both got out of the truck and walked around to the back to take out a giant stuffed monkey."

Sawyer gasps, and he stops.

I look at him, putting my hand on his leg and squeezing it. "Jake and I were never together, Will. I was helping him find a silly present for Sawyer that day. He was her boyfriend at the time."

"I still have that monkey," Sawyer grumbles from the back seat.

That monkey's a running joke between Sawyer and me now. Even though she and Jake had broken up years ago, she couldn't bring herself to throw it away.

"When I saw you together, how happy you looked, I thought…I just figured you had moved on."

When he looks at me, I shake my head. Of all of the times for him to have seen me. It was unfair.

"She never moved on."

"Sawyer!"

"What? It's the truth. You buried yourself in school and then your business and half-heartedly dated when I forced you to, but you never moved on."

Will parks in front of his house and turns to me, taking my face in his hands. "I never moved on either."

He leans forward and kisses me. His lips don't leave mine until we hear Sawyer clear her throat from the backseat. "Will."

He glances at her through the rearview mirror. "Yeah."

"I know people. You ever, even unintentionally, hurt Sarah, and there will be no place you can hide from me."

I turn around and gape at her. "Holy shit, Sawyer."

Will puts his hand on my leg and shakes his head before meeting her eyes again in the mirror. "Thank you for taking care of my girl. All I plan to do is spend the rest of my life making her smile."

Sawyer looks at me. "Okay. I approve."

I roll my eyes. "And you call me crazy." I reach my hand back to squeeze hers. "I love you."

"I love you too, babe."

When we get to his house, Will takes her bags up to her room while Sawyer and I talk by his car. Will is staying the night at my house, and my mother is driving us to the airport tomorrow. Well, today. When Will comes back out, he gives Sawyer keys to the house and lets her know there is a list of important numbers and things on the kitchen counter for her.

I pull her into another hug. "Thank you so much for doing this."

She shrugs. "Mama bear and I will be just fine."

It's late, so Will and I are quiet as he drives to my parents' place. He follows me up to my room, shrugging off his clothes before collapsing onto my bed. He tries to watch me undress, falling asleep before I finish. I crawl into bed and snuggle up to him, smiling as his arm curls around me, pulling me closer.

~*~

I wake before Will and am sliding out of bed when his hand wraps around my wrist. He tugs me back into his arms and kisses my neck.

"I love waking up with you," he murmurs into my ear.

I sigh and wrap my arms around him. "Mmmmm me too."

"I'm looking forward to seeing your place. Never been to Colorado before."

"I still can't believe you're coming home with me. This is crazy."

He lifts his head and looks in my eyes. "Good crazy or bad crazy?"

I smack his shoulder. "Good crazy. Definitely good crazy."

He covers me, his lips on mine. I want nothing more than to lose myself in him, but it's my last day at home, and my parents are downstairs.

I break our kiss, laughing at his pout. "Come on, Will. I want to spend some time with my parents before we leave."

He groans as he falls to the side of me. I lean over and give him a chaste kiss before getting up.

"I'm going to take a quick shower. You," I point as he starts to get up with an impish gleam in his eyes, "wait here."

He flops back on to the bed. "At least you aren't kicking me out this time."

I think back to my first day back. So much has changed since then. I shake my head, grab my toiletries, and head to the bathroom. When I come back into the room, I shiver when Will comes to stand behind me. He holds my arms and bends down to lick a drip of water I missed on my shoulder blade. I push him in the direction of the bed, ordering him to sit and behave. He winks at me and pants like a dog.

"You are such a dork."

"Whatever. You think I'm hot."

He groans when I drop my towel and walk over to my bag. I look back at him like, what? He somehow remains seated, eyes never leaving me, as I dress.

Once my summer dress is on, his eyes lift to mine. "I'm going to make you pay for that."

I walk over to him, ghosting my lips over his before I lick the side of his face from chin to brow.

His mouth drops open as he watches me walk out the door.

I look over my shoulder at him. "Bring it. Oh, and the shower's free."

He jumps towards me. I squeal and race down the stairs before he can catch me. I'm giggling when I walk in the kitchen.

"It's good to see you so happy." My mother beams up at me.

I blush and strain some orange juice before I go to sit next to her. She leans towards me and kisses my cheek. Will comes down not long after, his hair still damp from his shower. He kisses the top of my head before walking out back to call Sawyer and see how their first morning alone went together. He's laughing when he walks back in.

"What happened?" I ask, lifting a brow.

"I didn't know your friend spoke Italian. I feel bad for laughing, but after my mom called her a bunch of names thinking she wouldn't understand, Sawyer told her off. In Italian." He shakes his head. "Man, I wish I saw it."

"Are they going to be okay? That doesn't seem like a good start," my mom asks.

"Nah, they'll be fine. I think Sawyer might be just what my mom needs."

Our flight is leaving at one. We need to be at the airport at least an hour early. We spend the morning hanging out around the kitchen table, catching up with my parents and uncle Chip. My mom is going to drop us off at the airport.

"Are you going to move back?" my mom asks once we're in the chair.

I look at Will and smile. "Maybe."

Her face breaks into a wide grin. Will laughs when she pulls his face to hers to give him a kiss on the cheek. "You bring my girl home, Will."

She doesn't park, dropping us off at the departures. She kisses both of us, her eyes wet. We stand on the curb and wave until her car is out of sight before going in and checking our bags. They print our tickets there, and my mouth drops when I see we're both now first class.

Will laughs at my expression. "Sawyer wanted us to sit together."

I shake my head. We get through security and wait at our gate. Once we're boarded, I laugh, thinking how this all started a week ago. But not really. Will and I started that day he walked into my English class and stole my heart. We're landing before too long. Once we've collected our luggage, I pull Sawyer's parking ticket out of my purse. She had written down the row she parked in so we wouldn't have to try and find her car. Will laughs when he sees her Hummer.

I shrug. "She figures if she gets in an accident she'll just drive over the other car."

"What is her deal?" Will asks as he loads our luggage.

I pause. "She never told me the whole story, but she doesn't seem to worry about money. It's not something she ever talks about."

As we drive to my condo, I point out places along the way. Mountains, the office of the first business I signed in Colorado, Sawyer's and my first apartment complex, my office, and finally my home. I pull into my parking spot, suddenly nervous that Will is going to see my place. I wonder what he will think, if he will like it. Once we're inside, I don't have any time to worry about it before Will has my back pressed up against the inside of the front door.

"Well hello," I breathe as his lips move to my neck.

"Hey," he chuckles, pulling my dress up.

"I have a bed, you know."

"Here's good," he says, unbuttoning his shorts.

~*~

Will comes in to work with me the next day. It's surreal introducing him to all of my employees. At lunch, I drive him back to my condo. He tries his best to convince me to stay with him for the rest of the afternoon. He has ample powers of persuasion, but I want to have a meeting to discuss my move to Atlanta. I want their input. There are multiple ways this could go. I could keep the office intact and work remotely from Atlanta. I could forgo renewing the lease on the office space and let everyone work remotely, or I could sell the entire company and my new business pipeline to a competitor. I don't see the last option happening. I don't want to give up my baby.

When I get back to work, I call everyone into our conference room and discuss my plans. We discuss all my ideas and everyone getting to work remotely is the clear favorite. I was hoping it would be because with the money I would save on office space, I could afford to hire someone to take over the travel aspect of my job. In the past I used travel as a way to escape settling down and avoiding relationships. Now that I have Will in my life, I want nothing more than to wake up in his arms every day.

THE END...or is it?

Coming Soon

HER

You know her side of the story, now learn his.

"It was useless, I felt branded beneath my skin by a girl who left without even saying goodbye."

When Will Price was assigned a partner for a sixth grade class project he had no idea she would become his best friend. She eventually became so much more, and then, one day left with no explanation. Floundering without her, what does Will do during their time apart? And now that she's back home what will he do to make her his again?

Acknowledgements

First and foremost to my readers, thank you for taking the time to read something I wrote.

The idea for this book started on a plane ride to Tampa, Florida. It was early and our flight was super turbulent because of all this random wind up and down the east coast. It would have been a miserable flight if it wasn't for Kelli Rae. We clicked and talked nonstop the entire flight (probably annoying the crap out of everyone around us!). We shared our life stories and I am blessed to now call her my friend. Our conversations over rekindling old flames inspired me to write this book. To go from being the person sitting next to me on a plane to one of my biggest supporters, thank you so much. Muah Kelli!

My Betas, ohmygod my betas, Amy Surrey, Kristy Jamieson, Judy Greco, Elly Ruzgal, Lisa VanArsdale, Kate Dixon, Jenny Lopez, Angelique Miller, and Vanessa Brown (aka eagle eye). You guys mean so much to me and everyday make me a better writer.

Jennifer Short Benson, your love for my words and your passion made this book what it is today. I cannot thank you enough for everything you have done for me. You are like a one woman publicist, ahem scene whisperer, and indie author ninja.

Miranda Sue Johnson at Mommy's a Book Whore, you're my person. I'm pretty sure we were sisterwives or conjoined twins in a past life. We can have entire conversations in stickers. You are so generous with your time and support. I <3 you!

Yesenia Vargas, this is our fourth book together. You are the sweetest editor a writer can have. I am so lucky I get to work with you. Thank you so much for polishing my words.

Sarah Hansen with Okay Creations, your covers are amazing. Sometimes I just sit and stare at them. You truly have a gift and I am honored to work with you.

My family, you still love me even when the voices in my head distract me from things like; making dinner, cleaning the kitchen floor, or even holding a conversation. Thank you.

To my proofer, Rachel Ryan, thank you so much for giving me the peace mind to share Him.

To my writer friends; Nikki Mahood, Helen Boswell (amazeballs), Gareth Young (Spartan), Penny Reid, Karen Bynum, Rachel Walter, Emma Hart, Ross McCoubrey, Melissa Collins, Antoinette Candela, S. Moose, and Renee Carlino, and L. Chapman, your friendship and support mean so much to me.

To Maryse with Maryse.net, Kathy with Romantic Reading escapes, Jeannette and Kris and Nicole with I Heart Books, Mindy with Talkbooks, Kendall with Book Crazy, Louise with Hooked on Books, Cara with A Book Whore's Obsession, Danielle with Just Booked, Britney with Living Fictitiously, Emily with Rate my Romance and any other blog or page that supported me along the way.

About the Author

Carey Heywood lives in Richmond, Virginia with her husband, three children, and nine-pound attack Yorkie. In her spare time, she transports her children from one extra-curricular activity to another while maintaining her day job in the world of finance. Right now, she is probably eating Swedish Fish.

I'd love to hear from you!

www.carey.heywood@blogspot.com

@Careylolo

www.facebook.com/CareyHeywoodAuthor

Other Books

A Bridge of Her Own

Uninvolved

Stages of Grace